TRUTH SEEKERS

SEEKERS

THE MACHINE

BILL MYERS

TRUTH SEEKERS

THE MACHINE

B&H KIDS

Nashville, Tennessee

978-1-4336-9080-8

Published by B&H Publishing Group,
Nashville, Tennessee

Dewey Decimal Classification: JF
Subject Heading: ADVENTURE FICTION \
TRUTH—FICTION \ MACHINERY—FICTION

Literary agent for Author is Alive Communications,
Inc., 7680 Goddard Street, Colorado Springs, Colorado,
80920, www.alivecommunications.com.

1 2 3 4 5 6 7 8 • 17 16 15 14 13

For Paul Arroyo . . .

An esteemed man of God, beloved and honored,
who understands the vision.

And we know that all things work together for good to those who love God, to those who are the called according to His purpose.

—ROMANS 8:28 (NKJV)

Chapter One

THE DREAM

J
E
N
N
I
F
E
R

It was like a dream, but not really. I mean it *was* a dream but there were parts that seemed so real—besides the parts where Mom had actually died in real life. Does that make sense? I get those every once in a while, dreams that are more real than real, ever since I was a kid.

Anyway, in the dream Mom was driving our SUV up the steep, winding road to our home in Malibu Canyon.

Jake and I were in the back, sitting in our clearly designated seating areas . . .

Jake in his **WARNING: Biological Hazard Zone**, complete with empty Cheetos bags, crumpled McDonald wrappers (which had last seen action months ago), his wadded up T-shirt and crusty socks (which had last seen a washer longer than that), and don't even get me started on the last time he shampooed his hair.

I, on the other hand, sat in the **WELCOME: This is How Normal People Live Zone**, complete with breathable air and a place to sit without catching some deadly disease. (Jake accuses me of being a Neat Freak. Maybe, but it's better than being a toxic waste site.)

And where was our dear father in all of this? To be honest, he seldom shows up in my dreams—just like he seldom shows up in our real lives. Oh, he says he loves us and all, but what's the saying? *Actions are louder than words.* Anyway, I'll get to him a little later.

It was the same dream I'd had a hundred times before . . .

I was busy doing homework when I glanced up to see a monster truck coming around the corner in our lane.

"Mom!" I shouted. "Look out!"

"What's that?" She reached over to turn down the radio—one of her silly Country-Western songs about some girl breaking some guy's heart.

"Up ahead! Look out!"

But she didn't look out. And, just like all the other times, I saw the truck heading towards us, blasting its horn. I'm guessing his brakes had failed by the way he was scraping along the mountainside to slow himself. A good idea, except the mountainside was on our side!

Mom had nowhere to go. She swerved to the outer lane then tried to turn back, but she'd run out of road. We crashed through the guardrail and sailed out over the canyon floor, which was a good two hundred feet below. There was no sound. I could see Mom screaming but heard only silence—except for that Country-Western singer going on about his broken heart.

I spun to Jake but he didn't even glance up. He was too busy playing his stupid computer game. Then, just when the singer reached the line, *Why you stompin' on my achin' heart with your high heel boots,* we hit the water with a huge splash.

And this is where things get interesting . . .

In the real world, on the day Mom died, there was no water at the bottom of the canyon. It was September and the stream had dried up. And while we're doing a reality check, Jake and I weren't even in the car that day. Jake had been at the beach being Mr. Cool with a bunch of girls, and I was at home doing my algebra. (I know I'm only seventh grade, but besides being a neat freak, I'm kind of a workaholic.)

But in the dream there was plenty of water and the SUV kept sinking deeper and deeper with all three of us inside. Well, actually four, if you count the Country-Western singer who was now sitting in the front passenger seat, strumming his guitar!

Water poured in and quickly rose. Mom tried opening her door, but it wouldn't budge. She hit it with her shoulder over and over again, but the pressure of the water outside was too much. It began swirling around our waists and rising to our chests.

"Jenny," Mom shouted, "roll down your window!"

"It'll flood us worse!" I yelled.

"It's the only way. Roll down your window and swim out!"

"But—"

"Hurry!"

I threw a look to Jake who had conveniently disappeared. (Even in my dreams, he's a slacker.)

"Hurry!"

I rolled down the window. More water roared in, pounding against my chest and face. I had to turn my head just to breathe. Then I grabbed the sides of the open window with my hands, turned my head away for another quick breath, and pulled myself out into the water.

I kicked and swam until I grabbed the SUV and pulled myself over to Mom's door. By now the car was completely filled. Our faces were inches apart, separated only by her window. I yanked at the door handle. It didn't budge. I tried again. Nothing. My lungs started aching for air, but I kept pulling and tugging as Mom kept pushing and banging.

Still, nothing.

My heart pounded in my ears. My lungs felt like they were on fire. The outside edges of my vision started going white. Mom pounded on the glass. I joined in and hit the window with my fists. When that didn't work, I tucked in my feet, raised my legs and kicked it. Still nothing. My lungs were screaming for air. My vision grew whiter. I had to get a breath. I pointed to the surface and shouted, "I'll be back!"

She nodded and I pushed off, my lungs ready to explode. Sparkly lights danced through my head. I was losing consciousness, I was going to pass out, I was—

Then I broke through the surface, coughing and gasping. Cool air soothed my lungs as I gulped in two, three, maybe four breaths. I forced my head to clear, then took one more breath and ducked back down into the water.

It was dark and murky but I could follow the bubbles. The SUV had settled to the bottom of the river. When I reached the roof, I pulled myself over to Mom's side. She wasn't moving.

"MOM! "

I yanked at the door. I slammed it. I kicked it. I had to get her out. The door gave, ever so slightly. I pulled harder. It moved some more, then it opened with a groaning *CREAK*.

I grabbed Mom's arm and pulled, but she was stuck. I spotted her seat belt and reached down to unbuckle it. My lungs were crying out for air again as I pulled her from the car. But we'd barely started before we were jerked to a stop.

I turned and saw that something like a shadow had grabbed her other arm. At first I thought it was the Country-Western singer. I pulled but it held her tight. It was like a tug of war game, me on one arm, the shadow man on the other. And the harder I pulled—this was even weirder—but the harder I pulled, the more he started turning into this shadowy creature that kept growing bigger and bigger with huge, bat-like wings.

This is a dream, I kept telling myself, *this is only a dream!*

But my lungs were on fire. My vision was going all white again. This time I would not leave. I'd stay here and die with her if I had to, but I would not leave.

The pounding in my ears grew louder, filling my head . . . along with the song. That's right, the singer or shadow or whatever it was, had begun singing again. Maybe it had never stopped:

> I'll never let you go . . . you will always be mine . . . always be mine . . . always be mine.

Well, Mr. Shadow could guess again. Dream or no dream, he could not have her.

> Always be mine . . . always be mine . . .

My vision was totally white now. My mind shutting down. I could no longer feel my hands or my legs. I knew I was dying, but I would not let go. I loved her too much, I would *never* let go. The shadow thing may have won, but—

And then I heard a shout. "Augh!"

It sounded like Jake. But that was impossible. What would Jake be doing down here? I heard him again, even louder.

"AUGH!"

Chapter Two

THE VISITOR

J
A
K
E

Yeah, that was me screaming. But I had my reasons, which we'll get to in a sec.

The thing is, I'd been sleeping in my room, minding my own business, when I heard Jen yelling next door. The way she kept hollering for Mom, I figured she was having another one of her weird nightmares. Don't get me wrong, I miss Mom, too, but it's been ten months—you'd think Jen would start getting over it by now, or at least start having better dreams.

Anyway, I tried to ignore her and closed my eyes, hoping to get back to sleep. But she kept carrying on until my big brother DNA finally kicked in. Now it's true, we're

7

actually twins, but since I'm twelve minutes older than her, I qualify. And since we all know big brothers are supposed to protect little sisters—no matter what a pain they are (it's like a law or something)—I had to help. So, reminding God He owed me, I untangled myself from my blankets, threw my feet over the side of the bed, and fell over the mountain of dirty clothes I'd been collecting. (Hey, everybody needs a hobby.)

After ricocheting off a chair full of football gear and breaking my toes on a half-assembled skateboard, wall-to-wall video games, and an unpacked suitcase from last year's vacation, I staggered out of the room and down the hall into Jen's.

No chance of getting hurt here. The place was like a museum—everything dusted, scrubbed, carefully placed, and dusted some more. Well, everything but the talking chair in the middle of the room. The one wearing my dad's khaki pants, his white shirt, and had his talking face on the back (complete with glasses).

This, of course, explained my: "Augh!" that Jen mentioned in the last chapter.

It also explained how I woke her up from her nightmare . . . and caused the chair to turn and see me. "Oh, hi Jake," it said.

Which would explain my second, "AUGH!" followed by my stuttering, "D-d-dad?"

The face in the chair smiled.

"What's going on?" Jen mumbled, still waking up.

Dad's face grinned bigger . . . until he noticed my expression and glanced down at himself. That's when he realized he was actually part of an old-fashioned office chair. That's also when he shouted, "Robbie, what have you done? Fix this thing! You're scaring my kids half to death!"

More like seven-eighths to death, but I wasn't going to argue.

"Sorry," Dad's face sighed. "Robbie, our genius inventor, said he had all the kinks worked out of this thing."

I took a step closer and asked, *"Thing?"*

"The cross-dimensional folder," Dad's faced answered. "It's a new transporter for people."

"Transporter?" I frowned. "Like in those old *Star Trek* shows?"

The chair nodded. "But instead of traveling through space, it folds up our dimension like a piece of paper. And where the two pieces of paper touch, a person can cross over."

"That's . . . incredible," I said.

"Not really, just advanced physics. But I was supposed to transport to you while sitting in my office chair. I didn't expect to become *part* of that chair."

"Are you going to be okay?" I asked. "Does it hurt?"

"It's just a little confining," he said, trying to move. "As soon as Robbie transports me back to the lab, I'll be as good as new."

"That's good," I said. "No offense, but this is not one of your better looks."

Suddenly Jenny cried, "What's that?"

I thought she'd finally woken up and was talking about Dad. But when I turned, I saw her pointing to the corner of the room.

"What's what?" I asked.

"That shadow!" She was practically yelling.

"What are you talking about?"

"Don't you see it? The thing with wings!"

"Uh, the only thing I see is a talking chair that looks a lot like our—" Before I could finish there was a

SIZZLE-FLASH

from the chair.

I spun back to Dad who was suddenly rearranged. His face, which still wore the glasses, had dropped down to the seat of the chair. While his pants were now above him on the back of the chair, and his shirt was below him, wrapped around the legs of the chair.

"Robbie!" Dad angrily shouted. He paused as if listening to someone.

I turned back to Jen, who was starting to relax. "Is it gone?" I asked.

She nodded, but kept a careful eye on the corner.

"Maybe it was one of your dreams," I said.

"Maybe . . ." She obviously wasn't convinced.

"Hi, sweetheart."

She turned to Dad, then back to me, eyes widening. It was obviously another surprise.

I shrugged. "Long story."

Dad paused to listen again, then turned back to us. "Robbie says what you saw may have been something I picked up when I crossed through one of the higher dimensions. Whatever it is, it's made me unstable, so I'll have to talk fast. Your tickets are purchased and your passports are in the mail."

"Tickets?" I asked. "Passports?"

"Remember what I said at Mom's funeral? How I wanted you two to join me at the archeological dig here in Israel?"

"You're not serious?" I said.

"Of course I am. I just sent an e-mail to your Aunt Millie. She'll take care of all the last minute arrangements at your end."

"Last minute arrangements?" Jenny croaked. (She obviously wasn't used to carrying on conversations with talking chairs.)

"When?" I asked.

"In exactly sixteen days, twenty-two hours, and four-teen minutes." (Dad's a scientist. He likes to be precise.)

Jen and I stood speechless.

"Imagine," he beamed (well as much as a face on a chair can beam), "after all these years, the three of us together."

"Dad . . ." I stammered. "We've got a life here, we've got friends." I threw a look to Jen. "Well, *I've* got friends."

But he was listening to someone else again. When he turned back to us, he said, "Robbie has to transport me back, now. So . . . the two of you get to packing and I'll see you shortly. I can't tell you how excited I am—" But before he finished there was another

SIZZLE-FLASH

When the light faded, so had Dad. Well, most of him. He and his chair were a faint shadow and growing fainter by the second. "—to see you kids," he continued, his body and voice still fading. "How great for the three of us to be together. Just like one—"

There was another

SIZZLE-FLASH

He'd practically disappeared. "—big . . . happy . . . family . . ."
And then he was gone.

I looked back to Jenny. She took a deep breath and blew it out. And then another. The good news was everything in her room had turned back to normal.

The bad news was it would be the last normal either of us would experience for a long, long time.

Chapter Three

THE JOURNEY BEGINS

J
A
K
E

I'll spare you all the boring preparations like . . .

— telling Jen she didn't need twelve suitcases,
— getting tons of vaccination shots in our arms (which, of course, meant tons of arm punching from my pals),
— telling Jen she didn't need nine suitcases,
— trying to come up with excuses not to leave LA (for the record, no one bought the, "I think I'm hooked on air pollution" line),
— telling Jen she didn't need seven suitcases,
— and forcing me to take one suitcase. (Seriously?

After a pair of undies and an extra T-shirt, what's left? Well, all right, maybe a toothbrush . . . if I can remember where it is.)

And I'm not going to bother you with all the good-bye stuff at the airport—the way Aunt Millie cried and hugged, then hugged and cried, while all the time worrying we might have forgotten something (like they didn't have stores in Israel).

"And don't forget to floss!" she yelled as we headed down the boarding ramp. "Healthy gums are happy gums!"

No, I won't tell you all that stuff.

What I *will* tell you is the part where we were halfway across the Atlantic Ocean and Jen woke me up. Funny how someone digging her nails into your arm can ruin a good nap. I was about to complain, when I saw the look on her face. She wasn't scared, she was horrified.

"You okay?" I asked.

"Oh, yeah," Her voice was high and wavy like it gets when she's nervous.

"Are you lying?" I asked.

"Oh, yeah." She motioned towards the window beside her. "You don't see it, do you?"

"It?"

"The shadow thingie—the one from my dream when Dad folded dimensions into my room?"

I gave her a look. "Were you just asleep?"

She nodded.

"And dreaming?"

She shrugged, then asked, "Will you, uh"—she motioned to her window—"will you take a peek?"

I gave the expected big brother sigh and leaned past her to check out the window. Other than a few clouds there was nothing. "Sorry," I said. "Just a bunch of white, puffy clouds. Oh, wait . . . that one there."

"You see something?" she asked, her voice filling with fear.

"Yeah."

"Really?" She was still afraid to look.

"Oh yeah." I moved closer to the window. "If you look at it just right, it could be an overweight cotton ball. Or a deformed sheep. Oh yeah, there it is, big and huge and— OAFF!" (which is the sort of thing that comes out when you're punched in the gut).

Having accomplished my mission, I sat back in the seat to return to my nap.

"You didn't see *anything*?" she asked.

I tried to ignore her.

"Jake?"

I shook my head. Then, against my better judgment, I mumbled, "Why, what did you dream about this time?"

"I dreamed it was reaching out and grabbing the plane with its claws."

"That's nice." I began dozing off.

"Then it started shaking us."

"Uh-hu . . ."

"And then—"

I was just about out when the plane gave a violent jerk. Everyone lunged forward, including yours truly, who did a face plant into the seat in front of me. The plane jerked again, causing the lady on my other side to spill hot coffee all over my lap.

"YEOW!"

The seat belt sign *DINGed* and a voice came on over the intercom. "This is your captain. We're experiencing a little unexpected turbulence." There was another jolt, bigger than the last two. (Luckily, all the lady's coffee was gone.) "We should be clear of it in a moment or two. Please fasten your seat belts and remain calm."

It might have been easier to remain calm if the sixty-year-old hippy dude sitting two rows ahead of us hadn't jumped up and screamed, "WE'RE ALL GOING TO DIE! WE'RE ALL GOING TO DIE!"

This, of course, led to the usual shrieks and cries of mass hysteria. Then, as if proving his point, the plane tilted forward and began a giant nosedive so steep it would have made Space Mountain jealous. Now *everyone* joined in the yell-fest. I might have, too, if I hadn't looked across the aisle and saw some guy a couple seats over. Don't get me wrong, he was scared, too, but instead of screaming his lungs out, he sat in his seat with his eyes closed and his mouth silently moving. I figured he was either praying or exercising his lips.

I voted for the praying.

To be honest, it didn't seem like a bad idea. I mean when all else fails, there's always God, right? Besides, we're kind of a religious family—I mean half the reason Dad's an archeologist in Israel is cause he buys into all that Bible stuff.

So . . .

I closed my eyes and started explaining to God all the reasons He should let me live when, just like that, the shaking stopped. Eventually, so did the screaming. Everything quieted down . . . well, except for all the sobbing and hurl-ing into air-sickness bags.

I looked to Jen, who'd gone back to staring out the win-dow. Poor kid. All those days working on her tan had been a total waste. Now she was as white as snow.

"Is your big buddy gone?" I asked.

She wiped the sweat from her face and nodded.

"Good. I told you it was nothing to worry about."

"You never said that."

"Sure I did. You just didn't hear me over all your girlie screaming." I expected another punch. Instead, she just muttered, "Jerk." (The turbulence must have really taken it out of her.)

I threw a look across the aisle to the guy praying. He'd stopped and actually looked kinda peaceful. I figured that was a good sign, so I settled back into my seat and closed my eyes. Was it a coincidence—Jenny's dream monster grabbing and shaking the plane just before things got crazy?

Who knows.

But, just to make sure, I silently finished my own prayer, asking God to protect us from whatever we'd gotten ourselves into. Of course I was clueless about how impor-tant that prayer was about to become.

Chapter Four

GREETINGS

J
E
N
N
I
F
E
R

FIRST, THE GOOD NEWS

There were no more scary dreams on the plane. (The fact that I refused to go back to sleep probably helped.)

THE BETTER NEWS

Dad sent a helicopter to pick us up from the airport and fly us out to his dig in the desert. I'm not much of a complainer (for me it's just a hobby, for Jake it's a full-time career), but we were really tired and it had been thirty-six hours since I'd showered, changed clothes, or brushed my teeth. I could hardly wait to land and take a nice hot bath. After that, some time down at the pool, then ordering some scrumptious room service.

We were greeted at the hilltop landing pad by a young woman from India or someplace like that. She was dressed in a long, flowing sari and a purple-flowered shawl. She approached the helicopter, slid open the door, and shouted over the pounding blades, "Greetings! My name is Gita!"

Jake stepped past me so he could be the first out. "Where's Dad?" he yelled.

"Your father, he has many supplies to acquire for tomorrow's demonstration. He sends his apologies and shall return later this evening."

(My father. We travel halfway around the world and he's still too busy to greet us. So what else is new?)

I followed Jake out the door, squinting against the flying sand and dust.

"And you must be Jennifer!" Gita offered her hand to help me down. "It is a pleasure to make your acquaintance." Even though she was polite, I sensed there was something deep and mysterious about her. Very mysterious. "We are to be tent mates," she said.

"*Tent mates?*" I asked.

NOW, FOR THE BAD NEWS

She nodded and motioned down the hill to the dozen or so giant tents clustered together to form a little outpost. "As you see, there are no hotels here in the desert."

I quietly groaned. So much for swimming pools and room service.

She continued. "But do not worry. The porta-potties are nearby and we boil all the water from the well, so it is fit for human consumption."

I looked back to the helicopter, wondering if it was too late to crawl back inside.

Thinking I was searching for my luggage, she shouted, "Do not be concerned for your suitcases. A member of our team will take them to your tents."

"That's not going to be a problem!" Jake shouted.

"Pardon me?"

"The airline lost all of our bags!"

"All of them?" Gita asked.

"All of Jenny's." Jake lifted up his single carry-on. "I've still got mine."

As we walked from the landing pad, the dust and sand flew into my hair, worked its way into my clothes, and yes, even into my underwear.

"So," Jake said, "living in tents kinda makes it like camping out."

"In a manner of speaking, yes."

My heart sank a little.

"But 24/7," Jake said.

"That is correct."

My heart sank a lot.

"And over there," Gita pointed to a big open area where a handful of people were milling about. It was the size of a football field and surrounded by dozens of tall, metal poles. "That is the location of what we call the Machine."

The name made me a little uneasy. "The Machine?" I asked.

"That is correct," Gita said. "It is central to the Truth Seeker project. That is what your father has hired Dr. Robbie and myself to create. And tomorrow shall be our final—"

She was interrupted by a voice from behind. "Somebody call my name?"

I spun around and saw . . . nothing. Well, at first nothing.

"Down here."

I kept looking until I spotted a pair of red, high-top tennis shoes walking behind us. That was it. Just red, high-top tennis shoes walking by themselves.

"There you are," Gita said.

"There who is?" Jake asked, still looking around.

"You must be Jude," the shoes said as the right one rose in the air toward Jake.

"Uh, Jake," Jake said.

"Right. Whatever," the shoes said. "Put her there, pal."

"Put what where?"

"I think the shoe wants to shake your hand," I whispered.

Jake looked more confused than ever. But being a good sport, he slowly raised his hand.

The voice introduced itself as the shoe shook Jake's hand. "Dr. Robbie P. Ruttledge. We're gonna be roomies."

"Wait a minute," Jake said. "You're Dad's genius inventor friend? The one who cross-dimensionalized him and who's running this whole thing?"

"The one and only."

Gita cleared her throat.

The shoes continued, "Though I allow Gita, here, to assist me now and then."

Gita crossed her arms and scowled.

"Well, more *now*, than then."

"Where's the rest of you?" I asked.

"Yeah," Jake said, "you're a lot shorter than I figured."

The shoes chuckled. "Actually, these are just my remote robotic reconnaissance jumpers."

"Your what?" I asked.

"They are robots," Gita explained. "Robbie is most likely operating them from his tent . . . most likely from his bed . . . where he has most likely slept the entire day away."

"Not the entire day," the shoes argued. "It's only 2:48 p.m."

Gita scowled. "Are we not scheduled to take the Machine through a trial run at 3:00 p.m. in preparation for tomorrow's demonstration?"

"Gita, Gita, Gita." The shoes sighed. "That's a whole twelve minutes from now. You worry too much. You gotta go with the flow." They turned to Jake and said, "Ain't that so, bro?"

"Uh, yeah," Jake said. "Fact, I'm always tellin' Jen that exact same thing. 'Go with the flow.'"

Before I could point out that not once in his entire life had he ever used such a phrase, the left shoe rose and faced its sole towards Jake. "All right, Jack!" it shouted.

"Uh, that's Jake," Jake said.

"Right," the shoe said. "Give me five!"

They slapped hands or feet or whatever.

"So what's the deal with the Machine?" Jake asked.

"You're pops didn't tell you?" the shoes said.

Jake shook his head.

"That's what this little beach party is all about. Gita, let's take them over to the staging area of the Machine and show them our test run."

"I do not think that is such a good idea. There are still several glitches that are of concern."

"Relax."

Gita argued, "Should we not double check the dangers before exposing them to such a risky—"

"Like I said, you worry too much."

I don't know about Gita, but . . . *glitches* . . . *dangers* . . . *risky* . . . made it sound like there was plenty to worry about.

"I'll meet you there in five," the shoes said.

"Five minutes?" Gita asked skeptically.

"Give or take an hour."

"Robbie, I am very concerned for the safety of—"

"Relax. With me at the controls, what can go wrong?"

Gita said nothing, but the look on her face said she thought there were plenty of possibilities.

Chapter Five

THE MACHINE

J
A
K
E

"Four . . . three . . ."

Robbie continued counting down as he stood at the Machine's control panel next to Gita, Jen, and me. Actually, you'd never know Robbie was a geek. Weird, yes—but not crazy-nuts weird, or awkward-nerd weird. More like cool-sunglasses, braided-hair-to-the-shoulders, Hawaiian-shirt, Mexican-sombrero, and flip-flops kinda weird. One look at the way he was dressed and you knew he'd pushed being a slob to new heights.

Bottom line: I'd definitely found a role model.

"Commence firing sequence," Gita said as she pushed a bunch of buttons and switched a bunch of switches.

Robbie nodded and continued counting. "Two . . . one . . ."

We stared at the pedestal a couple yards in front of us. It was four feet high with an ancient oil lamp like they used in Bible times sitting on it. Above it hovered five or six ray-gun type thingies, each about a foot long that pointed down at it.

". . . and mark!"

Instantly the ray-guns began to glow kind of a creepy red—brighter, brighter, and brighter some more. And what cool sci-fi machine would be complete without even cooler sci-fi sound effects? Something like:

oozzza . . . oozzza . . . oozzzza

We stood in that open area, surrounded by a hundred metal poles, each one fifty or so feet high. And mounted to each of those poles were dozens of those ray-gun things . . . all pointed toward the field.

"Please, properly affix your goggles," Gita said.

We put on the protective goggles she gave us.

Earlier, when Robbie was giving last-minute instructions to his crew, Gita had explained more about the Machine and what it did.

"As you may know, sound is simply the vibration of air, which one does not hear until it strikes one's ear."

"Actually, one's eardrum," Jenny corrected. "Which is a tiny flap of tissue that vibrates and transfers those vibrations to our brain."

I shot Jen my famous your-brainiacness-is-getting-on-my-nerves look.

She just shrugged.

"That is quite correct," Gita said. "In theory, when these vibrations strike any object, they will leave microscopic imprints upon its surface—anything from pottery to ancient walls, even rocks. The Machine simply reads those imprints and plays them back."

"Like a digital recorder?" Jen said.

I gave her another look. But she'd found a new person to be teacher's pet to, so she totally ignored me.

"Very good," Gita said. "And not only sound but light, as well, since it also consists of vibrating frequencies."

"How cool," Jen said.

How boring, I thought.

Gita pointed to the pedestal and the ray-gun thingies above it. "Once those resonance amplifiers receive the vibrations from that two-thousand-year-old lamp, they are transmitted to this staging area we are standing in and will be projected as a three-dimensional holographic image.

Robbie shouted over to us. "A *superplasmatic* three-dimensional holographic image, if you don't mind."

Gita nodded. "Correct. In their hyper-realistic state, the images fool our senses into experiencing their reality. However, as mere superplasmatic holographic images, they never experience ours."

I had no idea what she was talking about, which naturally meant I had to fake it. "Right. You bet," I said. "That makes perfect sense."

"Of course, we are still unable to discern some color variations so we are currently experimenting with appropriate algorithms."

"Of course."

"Along with color density and saturation."

I nodded. "Goes without saying."

She rattled off a bunch more stuff, but since it nearly put me to sleep I won't do the same to you. Let's just get back to the cool

oozzza . . . oozzza . . . oozzzza

which kept getting louder as the ray-gun thingies kept getting brighter.

"Engaging holographic image!" Gita called.

"All right boys and girls," Robbie said. "Keep your eyeballs peeled. Cool stuff's gonna happen right about—"

But suddenly there was a new sound . . .

"Ooo-ooo, ahh-ahh, eee-eee"

and it wasn't coming from the Machine. It sounded like a screaming monkey, which just happened to be what ran past us and jumped up onto the pedestal.

"Maximilian!" Robbie and Gita yelled.

But the monkey totally ignored them as it continued its *"Ooo-ooo, ahh-ahh, eee-eee-ing."* Oh, and one other thing. It was chewing bubble gum . . . and blowing bubbles. Seriously, I'm not making that up. Then, just to make things even more interesting, it jumped up onto one of those ray-gun thingies.

Another voice shouted from behind us, "Maximilian, sweetie!"

I spun around to see a young woman dressed even sloppier than Robbie (if that's possible) running toward us. And way off in the distance behind her was some guy who looked a lot like Dad.

"Maximilian," the woman kept shouting. "Sweetie!"

But Maximilian Sweetie wasn't listening. Unfortunately, he was still blowing bubbles and swinging from one ray-gun to another, when suddenly, amidst all the screaming, yelling and

oozzza . . . oozzza . . . oozzza-ing

there was a blinding flash of light. No noise. Just a flash.

Once the light faded, everything returned to normal. Well, not exactly normal, but we'll get to that in a second.

"Hazel!" Robbie frowned at the young woman. "How many times have I told you to keep your chimpanzee away from the staging area!"

"I'm so sorry, boss," she said. "He didn't mean any harm." Patting her chest, she called, "Maximilian, sweetie. Come here."

Having done all the damage he could do, the monkey blew another bubble, hopped off the podium, and raced into her arms.

But the girl wasn't done groveling. "You know, doctor, I'd never do anything to jeopardize your incredibly fantastic work." She was laying it on pretty thick. At first I didn't understand, until I saw the way she kept gazing at Robbie and batting her eyes. Then I got it . . .

The poor dude's got some chick in love with him.

"Children!"

We turned to see Dad running towards us, all smiles. But neither Jen nor I felt like running into his arms and smothering him with kisses. There were a couple reasons.

Reason #1: We really didn't know him that well. I

mean, he was still our dad and everything, but we hardly ever saw him for more than a couple months out of the year.

Reason #2: Well, Gita probably summed it up best when she said, "Oh, dear me."

"What's wrong?" Robbie asked.

"We have no color blue."

"What?"

She pointed to Dad's blue work shirt. Well, what had been his blue work shirt. Now it was completely clear and transparent, except for the little white buttons running down the front.

She continued explaining, "Apparently, the flash from the Machine has absorbed all shades of blue within its proximity."

I looked around. She was right. There was not a single shade of blue anywhere near us.

Which brings us back to **Reason #2**.

"Uh, Jen?" I said. "About those shorts you're wearing."

"What about them?"

"What color are they?"

"Aqua blue. Why?" She glanced down to them and came to a stop. She raised her eyes back to me. "Are you seeing what I'm seeing?" she quietly asked.

I nodded.

"I'm standing out here in front of everyone in just my undies?"

I nodded. "More or less."

She slowly dropped her head to take another look. Then, after a deep breath, she raised her head . . . and took off running for her life.

Ever have one of those days? Jenny was having one of those lives.

But the fun and games weren't exactly over.

"Hey, boss?" One of the crewmembers standing at the pedestal waved at Robbie. The man wore a white robe and an even whiter Arab headdress thing that hung to his shoulders. He looked like one of those Arab sheiks you see in the movies. At the moment he was examining the ray-guns that Maximilian Sweetie had been using for a trapeze.

"What's up, Ibrahim?" Robbie asked. "How much damage did he do?"

"Actually, none."

"None?"

Ibrahim nodded and held out a broken piece of ray gun. "No chimpanzee could have possibly done this. It has been cut in two by a saw."

"A saw?" Robbie frowned as he stepped around the control to join him.

"That is correct."

"That would mean someone deliberately tried to sabotage the experiment."

Ibrahim slowly nodded.

"Perhaps it was merely a malfunction," Gita suggested.

"With my brilliant work?" Robbie said. "Not a chance."

"But who would do such a thing?" Gita asked.

"A good question." Robbie said. He looked at each of our faces. "A very good question."

Chapter Six

RENDEZVOUS

J
E
N
N
I
F
E
R

We were at the airport the following day when Gita put her Jeep into park, turned off the ignition, and turned to me. "Your father is a very great man," she said.

I bit my lip and looked out the window. "So I'm told."

We'd been driving for more than an hour and somehow during that time she got me to talking about Dad—especially about how mad he made me. I hadn't planned on saying a word. It just happened. And now it was like she was trying to defend him.

"At least your father did not attempt to have you killed," she said. "Not as mine did."

I threw her a look. Of course I was dying to know what she meant, but I wasn't in the mood. Not if it meant listening to her defend Dad some more. So I looked straight ahead, hoping she wouldn't keep going. No such luck.

"Even great men have their weaknesses," she said.

"You mean like totally ignoring your family and kids?" It came out before I could stop it and a lot meaner than I felt. Actually, that's not true. That's exactly how I felt.

This time Gita was smart enough not to answer.

We opened the Jeep's doors and stepped out onto the airport parking lot. It felt like a thousand degrees. I'm sure some of it was just my face and ears, which always get superhot when I get upset. Still, it was definitely warm and it was only 10:30 in the morning.

Earlier, back at the dig site, we'd had breakfast in the mess tent with the rest of Dad's team—about twenty guys and gals from all sorts of countries. The food was different, but good. Cucumbers, tomatoes, bagels covered in sesame seeds, and a thick, yummy spread called hummus.

Jake and I were hoping to spend the time catching up with Dad. But he'd gotten up early and taken the helicopter to some remote place. He left a note saying he'd be back in time for lunch.

"Yeah, right," Jake muttered.

I nodded. Neither of us would hold our breath.

Today was the big day. Gita had asked if I'd go back to the airport with her to pick up some superrich investor woman. They were going to demonstrate the Machine to her, hoping she'd help pay for the project. According to Robbie, they'd run out of money and Miss Moneybags was Truth Seeker's last chance to keep going.

"It's neat that she wants to help like that," I said.

"Help?" Robbie snorted. "The only thing she wants to do is make more money."

"What do you mean?"

"If this puppy works," he had said it'll be worth billions and she'll get most of it."

Now Gita and I were continuing across the hot cement toward the terminal. Even though she had tried to defend Dad, I liked her. A lot. Besides being smart and a fellow neat-freak, she was real considerate and sweet. And Dad hadn't been the only thing we'd talked about. On the way to the airport, as we approached Jerusalem, she had asked if I'd like to drive past what she called the Old City.

"Sure," I shrugged. "I mean if that's where Jesus was supposed to live, why not?"

"Oh, it's more than supposed," she said. "His life is historical fact."

"You mean it's in the Bible," I said.

"More than that," she said. "His entire life can be traced using historical documents that are not even in the Bible."

"Really?"

She nodded. "Will you find that red book in my file box in the back?"

I turned to the backseat and dug through the box until I spotted it. "This one?" I asked.

"Yes, thank you. Would you mind opening it to the place I have marked?"

I began flipping the pages. As I did, she explained. "It was written by a first-century historian named Josephus. He was a Jewish man who was definitely not a Christian."

"Here it is," I said.

"Please, read the passage I have underlined."

"Out loud?"

"Yes, please."

I began:

Now there was about this time Jesus, a wise man if it be lawful to call him a man for he was a doer of wonderful works, a teacher of such men as receive the truth with pleasure.

I looked up. "When was this written?"

"Just a few decades after Jesus lived."

"Wow."

"Please, continue."

I looked back to the page and read:

He was the Christ and when Pilate, at the suggestion of the principal men among us, had condemned him to the cross, those that loved him at the first did not forsake him for he appeared to them alive again on the third day; as the divine prophets had foretold these and ten thousand other wonderful things concerning him.

I took a breath. This was amazing. I finished the last sentence:

And the tribe of Christians so named from him are not extinct at this day.

"Tribe?" I asked.

She chuckled, "That's how Josephus viewed them."

I looked up from the book and saw a tall stone wall running along the road to our left. "What's that?" I asked.

"That is the Old City. And that wall is built upon the original wall, which surrounded all of Jerusalem during the time of Jesus. In fact, do you see that tower to our left?"

I nodded.

"That is built upon the Golden Gate, where we discovered the clay lamp we've been studying with the Machine."

"And the reason that's so special is because . . ."

"Because just under that tower are the remains of the gate that Jesus entered on Palm Sunday."

"Seriously?" I craned my neck for a better look.

"Yes. And off to your right, do you see those olive trees?"

I turned and spotted them.

"That is the Garden of Gethsemane."

"The Garden of Gethsemane?" I asked.

She nodded. "Where Jesus prayed the night of His arrest. In fact, those olive trees come from the roots of the very same olive trees that He prayed under."

"Wow," was all I could say as I continued to stare. "But with all this history around, how come everyone . . ." I paused trying to find the words, "How come everyone doesn't . . ."

"Believe?" she asked.

I nodded.

"It is not a matter of proof," she said. "It is a matter of faith. Whether they will trust Jesus to run their lives or not."

I frowned.

She continued, "Sometimes God does not always do what we would like."

"Tell me about it," I said, thinking again about Dad. Or Mom. Our being stuck out in that awful, desert place.

"But we must trust that His ways will eventually be best, even if we do not understand."

Once again, I said nothing, figuring it would just lead to another sermon. But no matter how I tried, I couldn't get her words out of my head.

That had been thirty minutes ago. Now the glass doors to the airport hissed open, and we entered the baggage claim area looking for Miss Moneybags.

And that's when I saw him . . .

The most incredible-looking boy I'd seen in my life. He was just a year or two older than me with dark hair, bronzed skin, and piercing blue eyes. Don't get me wrong, I'm not boy-crazy like the girls back home, but this guy . . . it actually took a moment for me to remember to breathe.

And to make matters worse, he was staring in my direction.

Of course I looked over my shoulder to see who he was checking out, but to my surprise, nobody was there. I frowned and gave a quick clothing check. Everything seemed in order—matching shoes, shirt right side out, no transparent aqua-blue shorts.

I looked back at him.

This time he wasn't staring, he was smiling. At me!

All right, Jen, I told myself. *Be cool, be calm. I'm sure there's a very logical explanation.*

"Miss Albright," Gita said as she came to a stop. So did I, but only after crashing into Gita's back. (So much for cool and calm.) I threw a terrified look to the boy, who cranked up his smile a couple degrees.

I glanced back to Gita. She was shaking hands with a tall, snooty-looking woman with gray hair. By the expensive dress and gorgeous pearls she wore, I'm guessing the giant diamonds on her fingers were probably real too.

"Good morning, Gita," the woman said stiffly. "I trust my valuable time here will not be wasted."

"Believe me, Miss Albright, it will not be wasted. How was your flight?"

The woman raised her head into the air and sniffed. "I've certainly had better."

She continued being rude and stuffy, and Gita continued being sweet and polite. I would have paid attention, but it was hard to think of anything since the boy had just turned his smile into a killer grin.

Stupid boy—what was wrong with him, anyway?

"And this is Jennifer," Gita was saying. "Dr. Mackenzie's daughter."

I looked to the lady and managed to croak out a "Hi."

Of course she totally ignored me and pointed to the baggage carousel instead. "There's my luggage."

"I'll get it," I offered.

"I should think you would," she said.

Grateful for something to do, I headed for the carousel. But it didn't help. He just kept looking at me and every step I took made me feel more self-conscious.

Stupid, stupid boy.

I was so busy pretending not to notice him (and trying to remember how to walk), that I didn't hear Gita pulling a luggage cart up behind me. No problem, except when I yanked the first heavy suitcase off the carousel and staggered backwards, falling rear-first into the cart.

Smooth, Jen, real smooth.

Smoother still, was when the cart took off . . . with me in it.

Smoothest yet, was not being able to get out . . . which meant a little shouting, a lot of arm waving, and a ton of people turning to stare at me.

Luckily, all good things (and nightmares) come to an end.

Unluckily, my ending involved slamming into a mountain of suitcases stacked against the far wall. Not a big deal, except for the part where they all tumbled down on top of me.

The good news was I was completely buried so no one could see me.

The bad news was someone started pulling the suitcases aside to unbury me.

The worst news was that someone just happened to be the blue-eyed boy with the killer grin.

"You okay?" he asked as he pulled the last of the suitcases away.

I pretended to be surprised that he thought something was wrong. "Who, me?" I asked.

He glanced around. "Well, yeah."

I sat on the floor looking like a total fool, while

pretending to be all cool and collected. "Oh, yes, I'm fine. Just fine. And you?"

He blinked, unsure how to answer.

I blinked, unsure how to breathe.

"Well, here." He reached down to pull me up. "Let me give you a hand."

After two or three tugs (for some reason my hands were not only cold, but wet and slimy), he dragged me to my feet. And then, in my best imitation of being a human being, I stuck out my hand for a shake. "I'm Jennifer Allison Mackenzie. Pleased to make your acquaintance."

He looked at me as if I were slightly mental. Who could blame him? But to help relieve my geekiness, he cranked up his heart-warming grin to mega-melt.

Still trying to impersonate a human being, I asked, "And you are?"

Gita answered from behind me. "Maria Johnson's son." I turned to her and saw she didn't look all that happy.

"Oh, hi, Gita," the boy said, pretending to notice her for the first time. "What brings you here?"

"I might be asking you the same question."

"Oh, you know, just hanging around."

"It would not have anything to do with Miss Albright's arrival, would it?"

"Who?"

Gita nodded knowingly. "I see. Well, please tell your mother, who I am sure is waiting outside, that we have picked up Miss Albright and do not need her assistance."

"Oh, okay. Sure." He smiled across the room to Miss Albright and gave her a nod. Then he turned to me. "I guess we'll see you around, then." (Insert Killer Grin here.) "Good-bye, Jennifer Allison Mackenzie."

I may have nodded, I couldn't be sure. At the moment I wasn't sure if I was alive.

With that, he turned and sauntered off toward the exit with me just standing there, watching.

"Jennifer," Gita politely suggested, "perhaps you should close your mouth?"

It sounded like a pretty good idea. When I found my voice, I asked, "Who was . . . that?"

"Jesse Johnson. Maria Johnson's son."

I nodded, continuing to stare after him. "And who is she?"

"Maria Johnson is your father's arch rival."

More nodding and more staring.

"She has been attempting to create a device similar to the Machine. And, like your father, she would love the financial backing of Miss Albright—to the point of stealing her from us."

When I didn't answer, she reached out and took my hand. "Come along, Jennifer. We need to be going."

I nodded and we walked back to join Miss Albright. Well, Gita walked. I sort of just . . . floated.

Chapter Seven

CATCHING UP

J
E
N
N
I
F
E
R

"Boy, have you kids grown," Dad said as we sat down at a lunch table inside the mess tent.

I'd just returned from the airport with Miss Albright and now, finally, it was reunion time with Dad. It was a hundred degrees inside, but I was sweating like it was a thousand. And it wasn't just the heat. A girl shouldn't be nervous around her own father, but I had what you call "issues." Other workers were sitting around other tables, but it was just Jake, Dad, and me sitting at ours.

"You guys are shooting up like weeds," he said.

"It happens," Jake said. "A little food, a little sleep, and here we are."

"Yeah," I muttered, "here we are."

Dad smiled across the table at me, "I'm sorry, did you say something?"

I smiled back, or tried to, and just shook my head.

Jake started digging into his plate of lasagna.

"So," Dad said, unfolding a paper napkin and spreading it on his lap. "What are you guys in now—fifth, sixth grade?"

"Seventh," Jake said without bothering to look up.

"Oh, right," Dad nodded. "Seventh. Time flies when you're having fun."

"Or dying from hunger," Jake said as he grabbed another piece of garlic bread off a serving tray.

Dad chuckled just a little too long (he was obviously trying just a little too hard). We ate in silence for what seemed forever, until he turned to me. "So, Jen, how have things been with you?"

"Fine," I said.

"How are you and Aunt Millie getting along?"

"Fine."

"And school, it's going—"

"Fine," I interrupted, maybe a little too loud. "Everything is fine, just fine!" (Okay, that was *definitely* too loud.) I threw a look to Jake who was oblivious to anything but stuffing his mouth. Then I turned to Dad who was trying his best to look pleasant.

"Sorry," I muttered. And I was. It's not like I was trying to be a brat. It's just when things build up for a few days . . . or months . . . or years, I guess all that resentment kinda bubbles over.

Dad looked to Jake who was still shoveling it in. "So, tell me, Jake, how do you like—"

"Fine!" Jake shouted. "Just fine!"

Dad stopped, stunned.

"It's a joke," Jake said through his mouthful of food. "It's supposed to be funny."

"Oh," Dad nodded. "Right, right." We ate in silence another moment. But in true adult style, Dad couldn't let it go. "Seventh grade," he mused. "Wow. So tell me, are you leaving the boys alone?"

"Yeah," Jake answered. "There's a couple bullies, but for the most part—"

"Actually, I was talking to Jen," Dad said.

"Boys?" Jake snickered. "Her?" (If my foot could have reached his shin, he'd have a broken leg.)

"Well, yeah," Dad said, looking at me and grinning. "She is getting to be that age . . . and prettier by the day."

I felt my ears start to redden.

"Are you seeing anybody special?" he asked.

I pushed a piece of lasagna around on my plate and finally answered, "Mom says no dating till high school."

"High school?" Dad sounded surprised.

I looked up and blurted, "I think it's a great rule!"

What? I thought. *I can't believe I said that. When Mom was alive that's all we fought about. And now I'm defending her? What is wrong with me?*

"No, no," Dad said, trying to backtrack. "She's right, that's a great rule. Fact, you might even think about waiting 'til you graduate from college."

Jake and I both stopped eating and stared at him.

"A joke." He laughed. "A little joke."

We nodded and went back to eating, which meant another awkward pause, which meant Dad having to try again. "That's a nice necklace, Jen."

I reached up and touched the little gold cross around my neck.

"Did Mom give that to you?"

I frowned. "No . . ."

"She didn't?" he said. "I thought—"

"You did."

"Oh, that's right. It was a gift for your birthday."

"Christmas."

"Right." Dad cleared his throat. "Well, thank you for wearing it."

I nodded and reached for a glass of water. Things were stressed to the max—except for Jake who was still shoving it in like there was no tomorrow.

"So, Jake, how's the guitar coming?"

"Dromphs," Jake said, bits of lasagna seeping out of the corners of his mouth.

"Pardon me?"

He swallowed, "I play drums."

Dad wiped his forehead with his napkin. "Wow, I guess I'm not doing too well here, am I?"

(At least he got that one thing right.)

He reached for his own glass of water and took a big

drink, then another. Finally he said, "Listen, guys, I know I haven't been the best father for you."

Jake and I kept chewing.

"And I know we missed some things along the way. Actually, quite a few."

(Right again.)

"I know how tough it is leaving your old life behind." He turned to Jake, "You, with your baseball."

"Basketball," Jake corrected.

"Right. And Jen, you leaving behind your best friend, Samantha.

I frowned.

"You don't have a friend named Samantha?"

"She doesn't have any friends," Jake quipped.

I bit my lip. Try as I might, I was actually starting to feel bad for Dad. "You must be thinking about Suzanne," I said.

"Ah, Suzanne." He nodded.

"But she's dead," Jake said.

"What?"

"Hit by an ice cream truck."

Dad looked horrified. "That's terrible. Why didn't somebody tell me?"

"'Cause I just made it up," Jake laughed. "Another joke."

I swung my feet under the table, looking for those shins. Sure, Dad was striking out, but at least he was trying. It might take more than a lame lunch talk to fix things, but at least he was trying.

Suddenly, people at the other tables stopped talking. Everyone in the tent came to attention, including Dad who rose to his feet. "And there she is now."

I turned to see Miss Albright had entered.

Motioning to an empty chair at our table, Dad asked, "Would you care to join us?"

Without a word, Miss Albright approached. Before sitting, she ran her finger over the seat of the chair and frowned.

Dad motioned to one of the servers who immediately grabbed a rag, raced over, and wiped down the chair. When he'd finished, she gracefully eased herself onto it. I knew right then and there that any chance of the three of us talking and working things out was over.

Now it was just Dad and what he really loved . . . his work.

Chapter Eight

A STROLL THROUGH TIME

J
A
K
E

After the eats we all headed outside to the Machine for the big demonstration. Dad was like a kid at Christmas—even with Miss Snooty Moneybags hitting him with all her obnoxious questions . . .

"And what do you claim to be the date of this so-called relic?" She motioned to the oil lamp on the pedestal beside us.

"Around the first century," Dad said. "About the time of Christ."

She checked her hair, which had about twenty coats of hair spray on it. Then she raised her nose into the air. "You have spent all this time on your archeological digs and that single artifact is all you have to show for it?"

"Actually, we've discovered several artifacts," Dad said. "Including what may have been a piece of Noah's ark, along with a button from that era. But we've chosen to use this piece first."

Instead of being impressed, she covered her mouth and yawned like she was bored. (I'm sure there was something to like about her, I just hadn't found it yet.)

"Excuse me," Gita called from the control panel. "Would everyone please put on your protective goggles?"

We all did—though the old lady needed help so she wouldn't mess up that perfect hair.

Dad turned to Robbie one last time. "Is everything in order?" he asked.

TRANSLATION: There'll be no mess-ups like the last time, right?

Robbie nodded as he kept typing at the control panel. Just to be safe, he threw a look to Hazel, making sure she held her chimp good and tight this time. There was something weird about the way monkey boy kept grinning at the old lady. Chewing his gum and grinning.

"Excuse me," Miss Albright asked nervously. "Is your animal okay?"

"Oh, don't worry about Maximilian," Hazel said. "He's just flirting."

"Flirting?"

Hazel nodded. "He has a thing for older women."

The chimp blew a bubble while raising his eyebrows up and down at her.

The old lady fidgeted. "A thing?"

Hazel glanced at him and laughed. "He's just showing off. It's only when he starts winking at you that you should start worrying."

Miss Albright smiled weakly and tried to focus on the demonstration.

"You're sure there'll be no reoccurrence of yesterday's event?" Dad asked Gita. He was beginning to pace.

She nodded. "We posted guards around the parameter of the compound the entire night. It would be impossible for an outsider to enter the camp and sabotage the Machine."

"Okay then," Dad said. "Let's begin."

Robbie nodded. "On my mark." He began counting down. "Five . . . four . . ."

Dad took a deep breath.

"Three . . ."

Come to think of it, we all took a deep breath.

"Commence firing sequence," Gita called as she flipped a bunch of switches.

"Two . . . one . . . and mark!"

The ray-guns above the clay lamp began their creepy, red glow, along with their creepy sound effect:

OOZZZa . . . OOZZZa . . . OOZZZa

"Engaging holographic image!" Gita said as she hit one final switch.

The air crackled all around us, kinda like static. For a moment the sunlight got dim, then suddenly everything turned fiery red. And I do mean *fiery*. Not just the sun and air, but the ground too. It was on fire! And it was moving! The ground under our feet was moving like a river of fire!

"What's happening!" Miss Albright shouted.

A good question and one I'd have asked, too, if the soles of my shoes hadn't suddenly caught fire. "Yeow!" I screamed, jumping around, trying to put them out. But, like I said, the whole ground was on fire.

"It's lava!" Robbie shouted.

"What?" Dad yelled.

"Molten lava!"

Gita looked up from her controls and shouted, "We have gone too far back in time! Before the clay of that lamp was clay, it was volcanic ash!"

"Fast forward!" Dad shouted as he joined me in doing the My-Shoes-Are-On-Fire tap dance. "The heat will kill us!"

"It's all an illusion!" Robbie yelled.

"It doesn't matter!" Dad shouted. "The images are so intense, our bodies think they're real!"

Robbie, who was also dancing, reached for the keyboard and entered a bunch of keystrokes until the fiery glow disappeared. Along with the heat. Or the illusion of the heat.

That was the good news. But, of course, there was some bad . . .

Instead of standing on hot, molten lava, we were sinking into a knee-deep swamp.

"Uh, Robbie?" Dad called.

And, instead of hot, fiery air, we were surrounded by a lush green jungle.

"Oh, Robbie?"

"Checking," Robbie said, as he madly switched switches and dialed dials.

"Dr. Mackenzie!" For reasons you might suspect, the old lady wasn't exactly thrilled. "This most certainly is not first-century Jerusalem!"

"An excellent point," Gita said as she studied the read-outs on the control panel. "We are still too far back in time."

"I'm not so certain." Robbie shook his head.

"Oh, I am," Gita said. "First, there were no jungles in Jerusalem at that time. And second, there were no—" she came to a stop, looking straight ahead.

"And second, what?" Robbie demanded.

If Gita answered, we didn't hear . . . not over the ferocious

ROOOAAR!

that came from an even more ferocious looking—

"Tyrannosaurus rex!" Jenny shouted. "That's a Tyrannosaurus rex charging toward us!"

One thing you can say about Jen, she knows her dinosaurs. Another thing you can say about her, she's never afraid to offer suggestions. You know, little, helpful things like:

"THEY'RE CARNIVOROUS! RUN!"

Now vocabulary really isn't my thing. But the way Jen took off, I'm betting *carnivorous* meant it wasn't the type of pet you tossed a bone to . . . unless *YOU* were the bone. So I took off, running with the rest of the group. I knew it was just a super-holographic whatever and it couldn't see us, but the last thing I wanted was to play tag with the feet of some giant creature who just happened to be taking a little jog. So we plowed through the jungle, its branches slapping our faces. For projected images, they sure felt like the real thing. And the hot, smelly breath of the Tyrannosaurus on my neck felt pretty convincing, too.

"ROBBIE!" Dad shouted. "DO SOMETHING!"

There was another crackle in the air and suddenly the jungle vanished . . . along with its obnoxious wildlife.

Now there were only people. Lots of them. It was like we were in the middle of a crowd. As they appeared, so did their shouting. Actually, I just heard one word, something like, "Hosa!" because suddenly there was a blinding flash like yesterday and everything disappeared.

Now it was just our little group standing in the middle of the staging area, trying to restart our hearts.

"Robbie!" Dad yelled. "You said you had this thing ready!"

"We did!" Robbie shouted, but he was looking majorly confused.

Unfortunately, Dad wasn't the only one yelling.

"Dr. Mackenzie!" the old lady bellowed. "You flew me half way around the world for this?"

"Miss Albright, I assure you—"

"You endangered my life with this . . . this carnival ride?"

"Miss Albright, if you would let me explain."

"No explanation is necessary. I should like to go home. Gita, book a flight for my departure tomorrow." With that, she turned and headed out of the staging area.

Dad was on her heels. "Miss Albright . . . Miss Albright . . ."

Meanwhile, Robbie had ducked under the control

panel looking for the problem and doing his own brand of bellowing. "Gita, I thought you posted a guard!"

"We did." She turned to a muscular Jewish guy who wore glasses and one of those beanie caps on his head. "Isaac, is that not true?"

Isaac nodded. "Yes!" He motioned to another dude in a beret. "Samuel and I stood guard around the camp's parameter the entire night."

"And you saw nobody?" Gita asked.

"That's right."

"Well, somebody was here!" Robbie said as he rose from under the board with a printed circuit in his hand. "And they replaced one of our microchips with this."

We all stared.

"That little thing?" I said.

"What is it?" Jen asked.

Robbie turned it over and over in his hand, carefully studying it. "If the camp's parameter was guarded the entire night, and no strangers were allowed to enter . . . then this little baby is our proof."

"Proof of what?" I asked.

"Proof that we have a spy, right here, within our camp."

Chapter Nine

MORE DREAMS

J
E
N
N
I
F
E
R

At first I thought we were back inside the Machine's staging area where everyone was arguing and trying to figure out what went wrong. But it didn't take long to realize I was having another dream—another one of *those* dreams. And on **Jennifer's Weird Dream Scale** of one to ten, this was definitely an eleven. Besides the usual weirdness like Jake wearing Miss Albright's expensive dress, complete with all those expensive pearls and diamonds, there were other clues.

Little things like:

— Gita and Robbie, standing in front of the control panel getting married, Gita in a lace wedding dress, Robbie in a wet suit, carrying a surf-board. And, of course, Jake was the minister.
— Two of Robbie's assistants shouting and accus-ing each other of being spies while battling it out in a fierce war of Rock, Paper, Scissors.
— Meanwhile, Dad and Miss Albright were danc-ing in the Nutcracker ballet—she was Clair, and Dad was King Rat (how appropriate). What was *not* appropriate was Dad wearing tights (which might have classified this more as a nightmare than a dream).

There was one other clue . . .

A black shadow flickering across the sky. I looked up and saw the silhouette of the giant winged creature. It circled high overhead and made no sound, which was probably why no one else noticed.

"People?" I pointed up at it. "Anyone!"

But no one paid attention. They were too busy danc-ing, getting married, and playing Rock, Paper, Scissors. I stared in fear as it finished circling, then tucked back its wings and dived . . . straight toward us!

"Guys!" I spun to Jake, who stood in front of Robbie and Gita, holding a Bible and quoting, "Dearly beloved, we are gathered here today—"

"JAKE, IT'S BACK!"

"—to unite this coolest of dudes and this awesome—"

"JAKE! IT'S HERE!"

I looked up. It was fifty feet above us and closing in fast. And the closer it came, the darker things got. Not just the sky. It was like the thing sucked up all the light from everywhere—the control panel, the wedding candles, Jake's pearls and diamonds . . .

Thirty feet.

There was nowhere to go, nowhere to run. Then I spotted a place. Under the control panel. I raced toward it, shouting, "HIDE! IT'S HEADING FOR US!

But, of course, I was wrong.

It wasn't heading for us, it was heading for *me*.

Ten feet away.

I leaped under the control panel just as the thing struck. Everything shook. Electricity crackled, sparks flew, but somehow the panel held up. At least during the first attack . . . which stopped as suddenly as it started.

I worked up the courage to stick my head out to see what had happened. The thing was rising into the air. Then it turned and dove straight toward me again. I screamed and ducked back under. The control panel exploded, pieces flying everywhere. As the smoke cleared, I saw it was right above me and I was totally in the open. I pulled into a ball to defend myself. But it did no good. The thing grabbed me and I felt its claws dig into my back.

And it began to pull.

I screamed, grabbing hold of what remained of the control panel. But it did no good. The thing gave a mighty flap of its wings and we began to rise. I squirmed and twisted, but it would not let go.

"JAKE! DAD! SOMEBODY!"

It started to shake me from side to side. I fought harder, screaming, swinging my arms, kicking. And then it spoke. The voice was human, a woman:

"Jennifer, wake up. Jennifer, you are having a bad dream. Jennifer—"

My eyes popped open as I kept punching and kicking.

"Jennifer, it is me, Gita. Jennifer . . ."

I slowed to a stop as the scene dissolved—and the light inside our tent slowly replaced the darkness.

"Are you all right?"

My eyes darted around the tent.

"Jennifer?"

And then I spotted it—a dark, swirling mist hovering right above us. Where its face should be were two red dots glaring down at me.

"It's still here!" I shouted.

"What is? What's here?"

It pulled back what must have been lips and sneered at me.

Gita followed my gaze. "Here? It's in the tent?"

I nodded, blinking, trying to will it away. "Yes," I gasped. "Right here."

She continued looking, but saw nothing.

It spread its wings, so big they nearly filled the tent. I saw its feet, its claws, they were reaching towards her.

"Look out!" I screamed. "Get back!"

But Gita wouldn't. Instead, she rose until her face was directly under it, just inches away.

"GITA!"

She tilted her head up towards the claws . . . and then she started to sing!

I couldn't believe it. I didn't recognize the words she was singing, they were in a different language. But I recognized the tune. It was from church. "How Great Thou Art."

The thing snarled at her, revealing hideous fangs.

But Gita only smiled and continued to sing.

The snarl grew louder, then shriller. It became an ear-splitting shriek, like it was screaming in pain, like it was being tortured. And then . . .

It was gone. Just like that. No shadow. No sound. Just my own heavy breathing.

"Did you see it?" I gasped. "Did you see that thing?"

She kneeled back down to me and shook her head. "No. But I felt its presence. I definitely felt its presence."

"What was it?" I was still trying to catch my breath. "What did you do?"

Gita spoke quietly. "I have an idea. If you would like to know, I have a very good idea."

Chapter Ten

MYSTERIES REVEALED

J
E
N
N
I
F
E
R

Twenty minutes later, the mysterious Gita and I were sitting outside our tent, staring up at the night sky. Being away from the city lights and out in the desert made each star sparkle like a brilliant diamond.

She'd also fixed us some tea. I'm definitely *not* a great tea drinker, but I had to do something with my hands, which were still a bit shaky.

"You didn't see anything at all?" I asked.

"Sorry."

"But you *sensed* something."

"That is correct."

"But how can you sense something that isn't . . ." I hesitated, then started again. "It was just a stupid dream."

"I believe it was far more than a dream." She took a sip of her tea. "And so do you."

Even in the warm night air I felt a chill ripple across my shoulders.

"You said the first time you saw it was when your father used the cross-dimensional folder to visit your room."

"Yeah, I was having a dream when he did it. Do you think there's a connection?"

She took a deep breath then answered. "Dr. Robbie was experimenting with it earlier this evening."

The chill grew deeper. "What do you think it was?" I asked.

"In my country we believe in many gods."

I frowned, not understanding.

"In my district most of us are Hindu. And my father, he was a very influential priest."

"Your father. The one who tried to . . . kill you?"

"Yes."

I looked down at my tea, feeling bad for bringing up the subject.

She continued: "While at university, I was given a Bible. I began to read it."

I looked up at her.

"All of my life I had felt there was something missing. And no amount of worshipping gods or goddesses seemed to fill it." She tilted her head towards the stars. "And then I read about Jesus. About how much His Father loved me, and how much He wanted me to become His daughter. Me. With all my problems, with all my failures. Me. He actually loved me. So much that He allowed His only Son to suffer and die for my every mistake."

"So . . . you became a Christian," I said.

"Yes. I asked Jesus to forgive me of all that I had done wrong, so that I would be clean, so that His great, holy Father could wrap His arms around me and hold me." She swallowed. I could tell she was getting choked up. "And what a wonderful Father He is."

I remained quiet. It had been a long time since I heard anybody talk about God like this. Not since Mom died.

She continued. "But as you can imagine, this news was not so well received in my village or by my father. Late one night, when he was worshipping, one of his gods told him that I must be put to death."

"God wouldn't say anything like that," I said.

"Not *the* God, Jennifer. *A* god.

"I don't understand."

"The Bible has another name for such imposters. It calls such creatures . . . demons."

The hair on my neck rose. "Like in the movies?" I asked.

"Like in the Bible," she answered. "Many believe such things are fallen angels—the third of heaven who rebelled against God and were cast down to earth."

I tried to swallow but my mouth had become dry as cotton.

"As a priest, my father unknowingly worshipped such creatures." She sighed quietly. "I know all too well what their presence feels like."

"And you think that's what I saw? A demon?"

She said nothing.

I shifted uncomfortably. "Gita, you're creeping me out."

She looked over to me and smiled. "There is nothing for you to be afraid of."

"Yeah, right."

"I am not lying. If you have given your life to Jesus, you have Him living inside you. His powers are several billion times greater than any fallen angel. Not only that, but because you are a believer, He has given you authority over such nuisances."

"Nuisances?"

She nodded. "To God they are even less than that. Jesus Christ has the ultimate power and authority. And He has given you, His precious daughter, whom He loved more than His own life, that authority as well."

I looked at her wide-eyed.

"It is true. Jesus said this very thing."

"But why me?" I asked. "Why am I the one who has to dream that stuff . . . see those things?"

Gita looked across the desert to the horizon where the sky was changing from deep violet to light purple. Dawn was on its way. "I am not entirely sure," she said. "But I do believe there is a connection to the cross-dimensional folder."

I turned to her. "How?"

"The Bible says there is a supernatural world around us. If such a thing is true, then such a world can best be described by scientists in terms of a higher dimension."

"Higher dimension?"

She nodded. "Many scientists believe there are many dimensions around us. Perhaps as many as twenty-two."

"I thought there were three?"

"Three is all we see. But just because we do not see them does not mean they do not exist."

I closed my eyes, trying to understand.

"By using Robbie's machine to fold dimensions, there is a possibility we briefly entered some of those higher dimensions."

"You mean heaven?"

"Perhaps, or some place in between."

I frowned harder. "I first saw that thing all the way back in California . . . and later when I was sleeping in the plane over the Atlantic Ocean."

"In higher dimensions, physical locations do not matter. That is how your father could directly visit your room from his office."

"So this dimensional folder thing is dangerous."

Gita thought for a moment, then shook her head. "No. It is only science. Besides, if Jesus Christ is your Lord, you are completely safe."

"And that . . . thing?"

"When I sang and worshipped God, what happened?"

"It freaked out and left."

"Exactly."

"So . . ."

"I am a Christian, Jennifer. Like you I am protected by the King of the universe. And when I worshipped our King, that creature could not endure staying in our presence."

"But . . . it was scary."

"That is the only power it has—to try and make us frightened. But we have another choice. We can put our trust in Jesus Christ."

I gave her a doubtful look.

"If you put your faith in Jesus, you are the one with the power. You have Christ's authority."

I took a deep breath and remembered Mom reading the same sort of stuff to us from the Bible. I looked out over the desert. The purple horizon was turning pink. "Well," I gave a heavy sigh. "I sure hope you're right."

"It is not a matter of hope, Jennifer Mackenzie.

I looked back to her.

"It is a matter of faith. It is a matter of putting your trust in He who never lies."

Chapter Eleven

ARGUMENTS

J
A
K
E

"Who are you calling a spy!"

"If the *kaffiyeh* fits, wear it!"

I glanced up from my third, or was it fourth, helping of breakfast to see a couple of Robbie's men going at it. They sat facing each other across a long table. One was Ibrahim, the guy with the robe and cool Arab headdress. The other was Isaac, the big Jewish dude.

"I am not one who takes something that does not belong to him," Ibrahim said. Then with a slight sneer he added, "unlike other people groups I know."

Isaac bristled. "Meaning?"

"Meaning, this very soil we are sitting upon was ours before you Jews stole it from us!"

"Excuse me? *Excuse me?*" The room grew quiet as Isaac rose to his feet. "It was our land long before it was yours!"

"Not only are you a thief who steals"—Ibrahim rose to his own feet—"but you are a liar." It was face-off time with nothing but the table separating them.

Isaac glared at him, while giving his jaw muscles quite the work out.

"Gentlemen!" Robbie called as he headed for them.

If they heard, they didn't pay attention. You could tell by the way Isaac reached for the knife on his table . . . and the way Ibrahim reached into his robe for who knows what.

"Gentlemen!"

The two men slowly moved around the table to confront each other.

"GENTLEMEN!"

Well, that did the trick. They both glanced at Robbie, who took the opportunity to wedge his spaghetti-thin body between them—so tight, he could barely breathe.

"We *(gasp)* agreed *(gasp)*, no hostilities."

They returned to their death glares.

"Dudes *(gasp)*, we're on the verge of a major scientific breakthrough." Robbie gulped in another breath of air. "And we're all working together, right? Just one *(gasp)*, big *(gasp)*, happy family."

Ibrahim sneered.

Isaac snarled.

"Okay, maybe not so happy, but *(gasp)* family, right?"

The sneering and snarling grew. If Robbie didn't come

up with something better, he'd either suffocate, or a fight would break out, or both.

"Besides," he wheezed, "I have this fantastic plan!"

They hesitated and looked at him.

"That's right." He swallowed.

They waited.

His eyes shifted back and forth, trying to come up with something, anything. "I have a plan to, uh . . . to uncover the spy in the next two hours!"

As an expert at telling tall ones, I knew Robbie was winging it. Poor guy. I wished I could help. But since he didn't need an excuse for not getting his homework done or for not getting his bed made or not mowing the lawn, there wasn't much I could offer.

Finally Isaac cleared his voice and said in a sweet, menacing, kind of growl, "How?"

Robbie's voice cracked, "How what?"

"How in two hours will you find the spy who sabotaged the Machine?"

"Oh, I have my ways. You bet. In fact . . ." Robbie desperately searched the room until his eyes landed on me. "My assistant here and I were just *(wheeze)* heading to my tent to finish solving the mystery—isn't that right, Joe?"

"Jake," I said.

"Right. So if you boys can just *(gasp)* take a chill pill, we'll have the answer very shortly."

Isaac and Ibrahim hesitated, then relaxed enough for Robbie to slip out from between them. It might have been my imagination but he looked a little skinnier and a couple inches taller.

"Great," Robbie said, checking his ribs to see how many were broken. "We're going to get on that right away." He motioned to me. "Let's get moving, Jon."

"Jake," I said.

"Whatever."

We left the tent and once we were outside I turned to Robbie and asked, "How exactly are we going to do that?"

"Do what?"

"Find the spy?"

He shook his head. "I haven't a clue."

"Really?"

"Well . . . maybe one."

Chapter Twelve

A CHANCE ENCOUNTER

J
E
N
N
I
F
E
R

It felt good to be alone. I know Jake loves to hang out with everybody and he's always "on," but sometimes, for me, I just have to be by myself. And this was definitely one of those times.

It was a long climb, working my way up the barren mountain above the camp. But the morning stillness was exactly what I needed. Except for the crunch of rocks and sand under my boots, and a faint wind blowing against my ears, everything was silent. Perfectly silent. I knew all the people below were having their issues about spies and the Machine and Miss Albright leaving today for home. And, of course, I felt bad for Dad . . . but, let's face it, I had a few issues of my own.

It's not a matter of hope, Jennifer Mackenzie. Gita's words still echoed in my head. *It's a matter of faith.*

I knew she wasn't trying to be mean or preachy or anything. And considering what we'd been through just a few hours ago, it made perfect sense. I couldn't get her words out of my head. I mean it's one thing to believe in God and all of that, but to actually have the type of faith she has? To trust God enough to go toe-to-toe with that whatever-the-thing-was?

But it wasn't just that.

I don't know when the doubts started. Probably the night of Mom's death. I mean, we spent all that night in the hospital praying for a miracle. And what did we get?

A dead mom. Thanks, God, really considerate.

Of course, everybody had a reason or excuse. But the point is, the great God of heaven, didn't exactly come through.

Then there's this whole trip to Israel. Not what you would call Jake's and my idea of a good time.

And now Dad's machine backfiring and Miss Albright heading for home.

Don't get me wrong, like I said, I still believe in God and everything. But to trust Him like Gita does? Like Mom always did? I took a deep breath and blew it out.

My eyes were starting to burn with moisture, but I didn't bother wiping them. Like I said, it was good to be alone.

Up above, I heard the cry of a hawk and looked up to watch it circle high overhead—so beautiful and majestic . . . and so alone. It gave another cry and for some reason I felt my throat tighten. Maybe it was the loneliness of the sound, or the way it kept circling and searching. Whatever. The point is, the tears finally spilled onto my cheeks and ran down them. I kept climbing, sometimes grabbing sharp or crumbling rocks to pull myself up . . . until finally, *finally*, I reached the top.

But instead of a fantastic view, I was met with a dirty, military Jeep parked twenty feet away. And stretched out across its hood, sunning himself was . . . a boy. Not just any boy. It was the boy from the airport!

He must have heard me gasp or something because he immediately sat up, squinted in my direction, then broke into a smile. *That* smile.

"Hey," he said.

"Hey," I said, giving my eyes a quick swipe. I was surprised, excited, and irritated all at the same time.

"What brings you up here?" he asked.

Too tired and startled to be nervous, I shot back, "I could ask you the same question."

"Yes, you could." *That* smile broke into *that* grin.

I felt a butterfly in my stomach. But I ignored it. "And your answer would be?"

"I come up here sometimes just to enjoy the peace and silence." He motioned to the other side of the mountain behind him. "My mom's compound is a couple miles away and this is a pretty good place to get away and think."

He looked out over the wind-carved hills and cliffs that stretched below us. The desolation was beautiful and heartbreaking at the same time. "Quite a view, huh?"

I pulled the blowing hair out of my face and nodded.

Then he added, "And it just got a lot more beautiful."

I blinked in surprise when I saw him staring at me. I didn't know what to say or do, so I looked away, already feeling my ears starting to burn.

"Sorry," he said, "I didn't mean to embarrass you."

I didn't say anything.

"People, they always accuse me of being a big mouth— you know, saying what I think. Sorry, I didn't mean to make you feel weird."

I may have nodded, I wasn't sure.

He slid off the Jeep and I glanced up to see him slipping on his T-shirt. "So," he said, "our parents, they're both archeologists."

The wind whipped my hair again and I pulled it behind my ear. "Yeah," I said, my voice sounding strangely like Kermit the frog.

"But there's no way your dad is as obsessed about it like my mom." He reached into the Jeep and pulled out the world's biggest orange. "Want one?" I shook my head. He nodded and started peeling it. "I mean, that's all she eats, drinks, and sleeps. Most of the time she completely forgets she even has a family."

"Tell me about it," I said, grateful my voice was starting to sound human again.

He stopped peeling the orange. "Really? It's the same with you?"

I nodded. "Sometimes Jake and me, we're like the last thing on his mind."

"Jake?"

"My brother. We're twins."

"Cool."

I shrugged. "Sometimes."

He started toward me as he went back to peeling the orange. "Wish I had a brother . . . or sister . . . or somebody. All I got is a bunch of foreigners and college students working for my mom."

"And your dad?"

"Divorced."

"Sorry."

"No biggie. I was just a baby."

He arrived and pulled the orange apart, offering me a section. To be honest it looked pretty good and since I'd missed breakfast and needed something to do with my hands, I nodded.

He handed it to me. I pulled apart a smaller section and bit into it. It was so juicy it squirted into my eye. *Terrific, smooth move.* It stung and made me wince, which made him chuckle. But instead of getting mad, I heard myself giggle, which made him chuckle a little more. In a way it was good, cause it kind of broke the tension.

"You okay?" he asked.

I nodded, and wiped my eye with the back of my dirty hand, which didn't help.

"Here." He stepped closer, "Let me." He took the sleeve of his T-shirt and gently dabbed my eye with it. "There, how's that?"

I nodded. "Thanks."

"No problem."

Still blinking a little, I squinted at him. "What's your name again?"

"Jesse. Jesse Johnson."

I nodded. "Right. And I'm—"

"Jennifer Allison Mackenzie," he said. "I know."

I nodded, pulling my hair behind my ear again. And you know that butterfly that was fluttering around in my stomach? Now it was doing cartwheels.

Chapter Thirteen

SUPER SNOOP

J
A
K
E

As Robbie finished adjusting the pressure cuffs around my chest and arms, I asked, "There's no way this thing is dangerous, right?"

"No way, dude." He began stringing cable from where I stood on a treadmill to the computer at his desk. "It'll be just like you're 0.3 millimeters tall—the size of a grain of salt. But that's totally bogus, because you'll actually be right here inside my lab tent, strapped into this SSCA."

"SSCA?" I asked.

"Super-snoop computer apparatus."

I glanced at all the cuffs and sleeves he'd attached to me. "And the reason I'm doing this instead of you is?"

"Don't be a moron," he said.

"Right," I nodded. "And, just for fun, are there any other reasons?"

"Someone has to run the computer, and since I'm the one who designed the program—"

"That leaves me," I said.

"Bingo."

"To do what again?"

"I told you, Jethro—"

"It's Jake."

"Whatever. You're the one connected to the mini-bot."

I nodded. "Right. Right." Of course, I had plenty of other questions. Little things like:

— Had he ever tested the mini-bot thing before?
— Would I be in any pain before I died?
— Where would they ship my body for burial?

But Robbie wasn't interested in boring questions like that. Besides, earlier, when we'd been outside and set the tiny 0.3 mm robot under the Machine's control panel, he'd explained the basics:

"This mini-bot is small enough to detect any human residue left behind from whoever took our microchip. By hooking you up to the robot, you will be able track those pieces of organic matter back to wherever that person has located."

Of course I would have appreciated him using a bit more English, but I figured I'd eventually catch on. And now that we were back in his lab tent, doing last-minute preparations, I was finally getting it . . .

"All right," he said, staring at his computer monitor, "slip on the headgear."

I reached for the combination goggles/headphones and slipped them over my head. Immediately I was surrounded by giant boulders.

"Woah!" I cried.

"Perfecto." His voice came through my headset.

"Where am I? What happened?"

"You're linked to the mini-bot, bro.

"What are those boulders?"

"They're not boulders, dude, they're grains of sand."

I reached out my arm and through the goggles I saw it was the mechanical arm of the robot. "Cool," I said. I turned my hand over and saw it was actually a big claw. "Very cool."

"Let's check out the sensors. Reach over and touch that grain of sand."

I reached out to touch one of the giant boulders. "It feels real warm," I said.

"Like it's been in the sun?"

"Yeah."

"Fantasmo. That means you're feeling exactly what the mini-bot is feeling. Okay, my man, you are totally and awesomely connected. Time to do a little hiking."

"Hiking?"

"You're on the treadmill here in the tent, so just start walking and you'll be moving the mini-bot's feet.

I nodded and took a couple steps forward. Sure enough, it was exactly like I was walking outside.

"How are you feeling?" he asked.

"Like I'm really here . . . or there. Or wherever I am."

"Terrifico. Now start looking for skin cells.

"Skin cells?"

"They'll be round and flat like a Frisbee. Look for the ones that did not come from me or Gita. We were the only ones at the control panel so any other cells would be from the spy who was there before us."

"How can I tell the difference between yours and theirs?"

"I've entered Gita's and my DNA into the computer. Anything that does not have our genetic code will glow—"

"A bright blue?" I asked.

"Bingo. Do you see something?"

"Oh, yeah," I said as I stepped around another boulder and headed toward something that looked like a glowing blue dinner plate.

"I see it on my monitor," Robbie said. "It's definitely a human skin cell."

"Oh, and there's another one, up ahead."

"Cool, follow it."

I did. It looked just like the other one.

"It appears you found yourself a trail, partner."

"And there's another," I said. "Hey, this is kind of fun."

"Keep following 'em. Eventually they will lead you to the spy's tent or wherever and—"

There was a roar through my headphones and a blast so powerful it nearly knocked me over. "Woah!" I shouted. "What's that?"

"Just the wind," Robbie said. "Be careful, dude. A tiny breeze to people is like a hurricane to the mini-bot."

"I thought you said this thing was safe?"

"It is . . . as long as you think like a 0.3 millimeter robot."

"Wonderful," I muttered. Of course I'd have appreciated hearing little details like that before I signed up for the project. But it was kind of late to bail now.

Another blast of wind hit and I ducked behind the nearest boulder until it passed. When things were safe, I stepped back out and spotted another skin cell. It looked like there was one about every ten or fifteen yards (mini-bot yards, that is).

"It's a wonder this guy's got any skin left," I said.

"Why's that?"

"He's lost so many cells."

"Not really," Robbie said. "Humans lose between 30,000 and 40,000 skin cells a minute."

"A minute?"

"That's 1,800,000 million cells an hour, 43,200,000 a day, bringing us to a total of"—I heard the click of computer keys—"roughly nine pounds of skin a year."

"No kidding," I said.

"That's what bloodhounds smell when they track people; their cells. And that's what we're following now. So keep your eyeballs peeled, stay out of the wind, and make sure you stay away from any—"

"Monsters?" I screamed.

If Robbie answered, I didn't hear. It's hard hearing anything over six giant feet

THUD-ing

the ground towards you. But it wasn't the feet that worried

me—it was their attachment to a huge bug the size of a giant tank. I quickly considered my options. And since there was only one that didn't involve getting stomped to death or eaten to death, I chose it. I spun around and in my best imitation of wanting to stay alive, I . . . RAN FOR MY LIFE!

When I finally heard Robbie, he was shouting through my headset, "That's not a monster, dude! That's not a monster!"

"Well, he's doing a pretty good impression of one!" I shouted.

"He thinks you're alive! Stop running, Jeb!"

"It's Jake," I shouted. "And if I stop running I'll be dead!"

"No way!"

As much as I'd like to stick around and explain the *many* ways, I decided to keep running. But the more I ran, the faster the thing closed in on me. Now it was just a few feet from my rear-end or tail or whatever mini-bots have back there.

"It's no monster, dude!" Robbie shouted. "It's an ant!"

I threw a look over my shoulder just as it lunged forward trying to crush me with its giant pinchers.

"It has no interest in you!"

"You might want to tell it that!" I shouted as I darted back and forth, the pinchers snapping, barely missing me.

"It's only attacking 'cause it thinks the mini-bot is alive. Stop moving and it'll probably lose interest."

Probably was not the word I was hoping to hear. I spotted a mountain of giant sand boulders beside me and ducked behind it. The monster was unimpressed and

SMASH-ed

through it. The impact flung me onto my back. As I looked up I saw the giant head and pinchers hovering just a few feet above me.

I tried to smile. "Hi there."

The head came closer and sniffed.

"Nice anty, anty, anty." To prove my friendliness I raised my robot arm to shake its hand or foot or whatever.

To prove its *un*friendliness, the pinchers grabbed my arm and tore it off.

"YEOW!" I shouted.

"It's only the robot's arm," Robbie said. "Remember, you're still safe and sound inside my tent, here."

"Sure doesn't feel like it!" I yelled.

"Here," he said, "let me turn off the sensors."

I heard him hit a few computer keys and the pain stopped—which was a good thing, because those giant pinchers were coming back for a repeat performance . . . only this time they were going for my head."

"Uh, Robbie?"

"Yeah, I see," he said. "Looks like its time to fly you out of there."

"Fly me out of—"

Before I could finish, a giant set of propellers popped out of my shoulders. And just as I was thinking, *now there's something you don't see every day,* I started lifting off the ground.

"This thing's a helicopter too?"

"Actually, a robo-copter."

Bidding a fond farewell to my cranky pal with the lousy attitude, I rose into the air. "Kewl," I said.

Robbie chuckled. "Thought you might like that."

After rising for what seemed forever, I asked, "How high am I now?"

"Almost two inches," he said. "Can you still see the blue skin cells?"

I looked down and squinted, barely making out the line of tiny blue specks scattered on the ground. "Yeah."

"Keep following them."

"How?"

"Pretend you're still walking, the robo-copter will do the rest."

I started moving my legs and he was right. If I stepped forward we moved forward, if I stepped to the left or right, we moved to the left or right.

"Outstanding, my man," he said. "Outstanding."

I heard more computer keys clicking. "What are you doing?" I asked.

"Switching to real-time satellite images. Gonna project the trajectory of those cells' route to see where it leads. And if my hunch is correct—" He came to a stop. "Oh, man. Not cool. Not cool at all."

"What?" I asked. "What's not cool."

"Hang on, I'm going to disconnect you."

"What? Why?"

"I see who our spy is."

"Great," I said.

"Not so great. He's sneaking out of the camp as we speak. Hang on, dude! This is gonna be a little scary."

"What? What's going to be—" There was a bright flash of light and suddenly I was falling.

"This is!" Robbie answered.

I looked down. The ground was rushing towards me at a gazillion miles and hour. And by the looks of things, it had no interest in slowing.

"Hang on, this might hurt a little."

"HANG ON TO WHAT?" I shouted. "WHAT'S GOING TO—"

SLAM!

Well, at least I had my answer.

The good news was, I was finally unhooked from the mini-bot.

The bad news was, it felt like I'd had my minimum daily requirement of broken body parts.

Robbie began pulling off the headgear and ripping the pressure cuffs off my body. "Are you okay, dude? Answer me. Jeff, are you all right?"

I rolled onto my back, grateful to see I was back in the tent. "Jake," I gasped.

"Whatever." He pulled me to my feet. "We've got to hurry before he gets away."

"What?" I asked. "Who?" But, of course, I had an even bigger question: "What do you mean, *we*?"

Unfortunately, I was about to find out.

Chapter Fourteen

BUCKLE IN

**J
A
K
E**

"Here." Robbie shoved a pair of ski goggles at me. "Put these on."

"What? Why?"

"We're going for a ride." He moved through the tent, around piles of electrical whatcha-ma-call-its and thing-a-ma-jigs to an even bigger mountain of junk in the corner of the tent.

"Now what did I do with it?" he mumbled.

I watched as he began digging through the pile, pulling out greasy motorcycle parts, microwave ovens, a satellite dish, three giant plasma TV screens, two snowboards (complete with snow boots—very useful in the desert), one chain saw (also very useful), and . . . Well, there was plenty more junk but I'll spare you the boredom, though the bagpipes were kind of interesting, especially when he pulled them out and tossed them on the ground; they immediately inflated and started playing "Amazing Grace."

"Not now, Sydney!" Robbie shouted at them, "Not now!"

The bagpipes gave a wheezy, defeated sigh and collapsed back to the ground.

There was also this cool-looking thing with a bunch of hoses hanging from it and a control panel in front that read, "Nuclear Power Vacuum Cleaner." But none of that interested Robbie. It took a while (and a few even stranger items) before he finally found what he was looking for.

"Ah, here we go." It looked vaguely like a riding lawn mower—except for the giant propeller blade attached to the top . . . and a rocket engine bolted to each side.

"What are you doing with that?" I asked.

Standing on his toes to check the propeller, he said, "We are going to catch a spy."

There was that word again . . . *We.*

Before I could question him, the door flew open and there stood Hazel, complete with Monkey Boy, the gum-chewing chimp, on her shoulder. "And how is our wonderful and ever-so-beautiful day going so far, Dr. Robbie?"

"You're just in time," Robbie said without looking at her.

"Oh goodie. I just love to assist you in your great and awesome plans!" I could hear her batting her eyelashes all the way across the tent.

"Yeah, whatever," Robbie said as he inspected the engines.

While he spoke, the chimpanzee hopped off Hazel's shoulder and

Ooo-ooo, ahh-ahh, ee-ee-ed

all the way across the tent until he crawled up to Robbie's computer keyboard.

Seeing the contraption, Hazel asked, "Oh, and are we going to test the ever-soar gyromower again?" (To be honest I didn't know if she meant, *ever-soar* or *ever-sore*. Either way, I guessed it wouldn't be that much fun.) "You know what happened the last time we tested it." (Now I knew it wouldn't.)

"Old news," Robbie said. He bent over to check the two seats. "Besides, aren't the first test riders out of the hospital now?"

"Yes . . . at least the one who survived."

"Great." He rummaged around another pile and pulled out two football helmets and two backpacks. "I want you to stay and run the computer for me. Give us the real-time coordinates while Jude and I track down the spy."

"Oh, goodie!" Hazel clapped her hands. "Maximilian, won't this be fun?"

The chimp would have answered but he was too busy checking out the computer keyboard.

Hazel moved beside him, slipped on the computer headset, and asked Robbie, "How much fuel do you have?"

"With the enlarged tanks, we'll be able to go ten minutes."

"Amazing." Hazel turned to me and sighed dreamily, "Isn't he the most amazing?"

Robbie handed me one of the helmets. "Here." And then a backpack. "You'll need this too."

"But"—I swallowed nervously—"you said it would only take ten minutes."

"It might get a little bumpy."

"How's a backpack going to stop things from getting bumpy?"

Hazel burst out laughing.

Robbie just smiled as he slipped on his own backpack and helmet. "I like you kid. You got a real sense of humor. Come on." He pushed the gyromower across the tent and out into the hot desert sun.

I cleared my throat. "Are you really sure this thing is safe?"

He pressed the starter button and the giant overhead blades began to turn "I made it," he said. "Of course it's safe."

Somehow that didn't make me feel better.

He motioned to the backseat. "Hop on, we haven't much time. You'll be my onboard navigator."

The blades spun faster.

"I don't know anything about navigating," I said.

"You're not afraid, are you?"

"No, of course—"

"'Cause you sound afraid."

"No, I'm not afraid. Don't be stupid, why would I be afraid?"

"Then get on and buckle in."

Reluctantly, I obeyed. (Sometimes being supercool can be super-suicidal.)

The propeller kicked up sand all around as he threw his leg over the front seat and adjusted his helmet microphone. "Test one, test two. Hazel, can you hear me?"

Her voice crackled through the headphones of our helmets. "Roger that, Dr. Robbie. Maximilian and I hear you loud and clear . . . and such a deep, manly voice it is."

Robbie turned back to me. "You buckled in?"

I nodded.

"Grab my waist and hang on."

"Listen," I said. "Maybe you should get someone else to—"

He revved the engine and we slowly rose off the ground. And, just as I started thinking, *Hm, maybe this won't be so bad after all,* he flipped a single switch, fired the rockets, and we

wooooshh-ed

up into the air like something from Cape Canaveral.

Chapter Fifteen

A LITTLE DRIVE

J
E
N
N
I
F
E
R

As I kept talking to Jesse, I slowly loosened up. It felt good to start feeling like a semi-intelligent human being—although it would have been easier if my stomach didn't keep doing backflips every time he smiled. But all those years of trying to stay calm and collected around the world's most irritating brother paid off. Believe it or not, I succeeded in staying the tiniest bit rational, at least enough to see that Jesse was also pretty nervous.

Amazing. Mr. Cool with the piercing blue eyes and heartbreaker smile was nervous talking to me. *Me.* Unbelievable. To be honest, it was kinda cute the way he kept glancing around. I'd never had that effect on a boy before. Not only did it make me feel good, but it made him seem all the sweeter.

"So." He fidgeted slightly. "What do you think of the country so far?"

"The desert's a little warm," I said.

"You can say that again." He chuckled nervously.

I nodded.

He nodded.

He pushed a rock around with his toe then glanced up, looking past me. Poor guy. He had it bad. He was obviously trying to think of something to say, so I helped him out. "You come up here often?" I asked.

He nodded. "Like I said, it gives me a place to think."

"Oh, that's right." I bit my lip for being so lame.

"What about you?" he asked.

"I just got here, remember?"

"Oh, right." He glanced away.

"Aren't you a little young for driving?" I asked.

He shook his head. "Out here in the desert, no one cares."

More silence. There was nothing but the wind. Then, just when I was about to open my mouth, unsure what to say but pretty sure it would be something even more stupid, I heard: "Johnson! Johnson, where are you?"

I turned and saw one of Dad's workers staggering up the hill behind me. He was huffing and puffing with skinny toothpick legs and a giant beach ball of a body.

"Up here!" Jesse called. "You're late!"

Suddenly I got a sinking feeling. He wasn't nervous about talking to me, he was nervous waiting for this person.

The man spotted me and demanded, "What's she doing here?"

"This is Jennifer Mackenzie," Jesse said. "She's—"

"I know who she is. What's she doing here?"

"We were just talking."

"Yeah, well, talk time is over." The man brushed past me and headed for the Jeep. "Let's get out of here."

Jesse nodded, started to turn, then turned back to me. "It was good talking to you, Jennifer."

I nodded, feeling my throat tighten. It was stupid, I know—but all this time I'd thought *I* was the reason he was so awkward and uneasy.

"Come on!" the man shouted as he climbed behind the wheel. "Let's go!"

Jesse moved to join him. As he climbed onboard and dropped into the seat, he turned back to me and called, "We'll talk again, okay?"

I gave my eyes a quick brush and nodded.

The driver fired up the Jeep but, just before he put it into gear, there was the world's biggest

woooosh

coming from the camp below. I spun around to see something shooting straight at us. Well, not exactly straight—it did a few zigs and zags along the way, but it was definitely heading our way!

"What is it?" Jesse yelled to the driver.

The man squinted then shouted, "A guided missile!"

"A what?"

"That crazy Robbie just fired a missile at us!" The driver threw the Jeep into gear. "Let's get out of here!"

"Wait!" Jesse shouted. "What about the girl?"

"That's her problem!" The man stepped on the gas and they peeled out.

"NO!" Jesse grabbed the wheel.

"What are you doing?"

"We can't just leave her here!"

"Let go!" The man fought him, but Jesse yanked the wheel until the Jeep slid into a circle.

"If it hits here, it'll kill her!" he shouted.

Angry and frustrated, the driver slammed on the brakes and skidded to a stop. "Come on!" he yelled at me "Get in!"

I glanced back at the missile and for the briefest second I thought I heard a scream. Weirder yet, it almost sounded like Jake.

"Now!" the man shouted.

"Hurry!" Jesse yelled.

I raced for the Jeep and arrived just as the driver took off. It would have been easier if he'd waited until I got in, but he obviously didn't want to hang around and get blown up. Jesse stretched out his hand. "Here!" he shouted. "Grab hold!" I took it and he pulled me onboard. I tried moving to the back, as we picked up speed and the Jeep bounced across the rocky ground. I almost made it until we hit a huge boulder and the Jeep went sailing into the air.

"Hang on!" Jesse shouted.

I'd have preferred hearing the warning *before* we hit the boulder instead of *after*—since it was a little embarrassing landing head-first into the back floorboard, with my rear sticking straight up.

I struggled and turned around just as the driver shouted, "Where's the missile?"

"Uh-oh," Jesse said.

"Uh-oh, what?"

"It's locked onto us!"

I followed his gaze to see the thing was above us now, whizzing back and forth all over the place. "That's not a guided missile!" I shouted.

"What is it?" the driver yelled.

Jesse answered, "It's a guided . . . a guided—"

"Lawnmower!" I cried.

"A what?"

Jesse shouted, "It looks like a rocket-powered lawnmower!"

"Who would be crazy enough to fly such a thing?"

It swooped closer and Jesse yelled, "It's the Robbie inventor guy. And some kid!"

"That's no kid!" I shouted. "That's my—"

"Jen!" Jake yelled from the lawnmower. "Is that you?"

I closed my eyes, not believing what I saw. I shook my head and reopened them. It didn't help. "What are you doing up there?" I shouted.

"What are you doing down there?"

"Long story!"

"Me too!"

Jake sat in the backseat and Robbie sat up front, steering and yelling into the mouthpiece of his helmet. "I don't care how curious Maximilian is! He can not play with the"—the lawnmower veered hard to the right, then to the left, then to the right—"keyboard!"

Jake shouted down to me. "They've got the microchip!"

"The what?" I yelled.

"You're with the guys who stole the part from Dad's machine!"

I turned to Jesse just as the driver cranked the wheel hard, trying to lose them. No luck. The lawnmower stayed right on our tail (more or less).

"Robbie!" Jake yelled. "I think I'm going to hurl!"

But Robbie was too busy shouting into his mouthpiece to answer. "Get him away from the controls! Hazel, do you hear me?"

But the lawnmower just kept weaving. Then to make things more interesting, it began bucking.

Jake yelled down at us. "We've got you surrounded! Throw down the microchip and come out with your hands up!" (My brother had obviously seen too many police shows.)

As we sped down the back side of the hill, the driver seemed to hit every bump, rut, and rock he could find.

Again Robbie shouted into his headset. "Now, Hazel! Get the chimp away from the controls and—"

Suddenly the front of the lawnmower rose and the whole thing shot straight up into the air . . . with both Jake and Robbie screaming:

!

H

H

H

A

I shouted at the driver. "Are you the spy? Are you the guy that ruined my dad's experiment?"

He ignored me and I turned my glare on Jesse. "Is he?"

But Jesse had no time to answer because, as we all know, what goes up must come down. And by the look and sound of things, Robbie and Jake were coming down right on top of

A

H

H

H

!

us.

"MAYDAY! MAYDAY!" Robbie yelled.

"PULL UP!" Jake shouted. "PULL UP!

"I CAN'T!" Robbie yelled. "ABORT! ABORT!"

"WHAT?"

"PULL THE RIP CORD ON YOUR PARACHUTE!"

"WHAT RIP CORD? WHAT PARACHUTE? ALL I HAVE IS THIS STUPID BACKPACK!"

"PULL ITS CORD!"

I saw Jake pull at something. Robbie did the same. Suddenly they both flew off the lawnmower. Parachutes unraveled behind each of them and billowed open above their heads. Within seconds they were gently floating to the ground. I would have breathed a sigh of relief except the lawnmower was still heading for us.

The driver slammed on the brakes and the Jeep went into a sliding skid—great fun until we hit another one of those pesky boulders. But instead of sending the Jeep flying into the air, it sent all of us flying out of the Jeep.

The sand we landed in was pretty soft.

The rock wall the Jeep hit was not—which explains why it burst into flames.

I was pretty dazed and it took a moment for me to roll over and crawl onto my hands and knees. By then, Jake was already at my side.

"You okay, sis? You all right?"

I shook my head, trying to clear it. Eventually, Jake helped me to my feet.

"Whhh—" I spit out a mouthful of sand and tried again. "Where are they?"

"Who?"

"Jesse and—"

"They're gone."

I frowned.

He motioned to the bottom of the hill where Jesse and the driver were running for their lives.

"It'll be the last we see of them," he said. "You can be glad for that."

I watched silently, anything but glad. Mad? You bet. Real mad. But there was another part of me—not glad, not mad . . . but sad.

Real sad.

Chapter Sixteen

A REVELATION

J
A
K
E

Jen was pretty steamed. And for once in her life, it wasn't at me. That was the good news.

That bad news was . . . she was steamed at God.

Why did He almost get us killed?

Why did He let someone ruin Dad's machine?

Why did He let Mom die?

Why? Why? Why?

Of course, I didn't have any answers. The best I figured, nobody did. But that didn't stop her from asking. I knew she was just letting off steam, but I also knew part of her was serious. Real serious.

"Come on, Jen," I said as we headed towards the

central lab tent. "Just let it go. In case you haven't noticed your arm's too short to box with God."

But she wouldn't let it go. Being her usual, bull-headed self, she refused to listen. She just went on and on . . . and on some more. It wasn't until we finally stepped inside the tent that she finally settled down. A little.

Of course, we were expecting to tell Dad our latest "adventure" (better known as "catastrophe") but, as usual, he was too busy to hear. Oh, he pretended to listen, but you know how it is when parents pretend—it's like they're on autopilot and rattle off the usual one-size-fits-all answers.

Not that Dad didn't have a good reason. (He always has a good reason.) And, to be honest, this one was pretty cool.

When we walked inside he had computers, books, maps, and charts scattered all over this big, round, glass table that was lit from underneath. Behind him was a giant TV screen. And by the look of his crumpled clothes and messy hair, he'd been working all night and into the morning.

"Hey, Dad," I said.

"Uh-huh," he said.

"We almost got killed," I said.

"You don't say," he said.

"Yeah, fact we could be dead, right now, this very second."

"That's nice."

(See what I mean about autopilot?)

I sighed and threw a look over to Jen, who was already commencing one of her world-famous eye rolls. I decided to find a subject more to *his* liking. "So what have you been up to?"

"This is the most fantastic thing, Jake." He stared at his charts, never bothering to look up (but at least he got my name right). "Do you remember our experience inside the Machine yesterday?"

"Uh, yeah," I said, "a little hard to forget."

But he was too caught up to appreciate my sarcasm.

"And that brief moment we were in the crowd of people—do you remember?" he asked.

It was Jen's turn for sarcasm. "Was that before or after the Jurassic Park ride?"

Like I said, he was too busy to appreciate our humor. "Do you remember what they were wearing?" he asked.

I shook my head. "We were kinda busy running for our lives."

He reached to one of the computer keyboards in the table and typed a quick code. "We were only there a moment," he said "But take a look."

An image flickered on the screen behind him. It was exactly what we'd seen—a crowd of people all shouting and waving. It lasted for, like, two seconds. He hit Repeat, and then Freeze to hold the image.

"See their clothes?" he asked.

"Robes," I said.

"Precisely." He typed in another code and the image zoomed into a close-up of one woman wearing a robe and some sort of scarf on her head. "As suspected, because of our clay lamp's age, we're looking at something around the first century."

Jen took a step closer to the screen. Even though she

was angry, she was definitely interested. "You said somewhere around the time of Christ."

"Yes!" Dad was getting even more excited. "And this"—he typed in more code—"take a look at this!"

The pictured tilted up toward the sky. Everything was blurry and overexposed from the sun, but you could still make out what looked like a bunch of raised hands.

"Do you see that?" Dad said. "Do you see it?"

"Hands," I said.

"Waving?" Jen added.

"Yes, yes, but in those hands! Do you see what's in one of those hands?" He typed more code and the picture zoomed in tighter, making it even blurrier.

Jen and I squinted but it was impossible to tell what he was talking about.

"A palm branch!" Dad grabbed an electric pencil and quickly outlined something on the built-in table monitor, which transferred to the big screen behind him. "See! Right there. A palm branch! A palm branch!"

"Okay," I said, "a palm branch." I looked at Jen, but she just shrugged.

"Isn't that fantastic?" Dad sounded like he'd just won the lotto as he typed more stuff into the keyboard. "Now listen to this. This is what they were shouting." He hit a final key and the image on the big screen started playing again, this time with sound. You could actually hear the people cheering—and then a word or name or something that sounded like "hosa."

"Did you hear that?" Dad cried. "Did you hear what they shouted?"

He played it again. Again there was the waving and cheering and shouting of "hosa." He stopped it and played it again. And again. Finally he hit Pause and turned to us beaming like a cat who swallowed a canary . . . or an entire bird store.

I cleared my throat. "Hosa?" I asked.

He looked at me eagerly.

"Sorry," I said. "I don't get it."

He turned to Jen, obviously hoping for a better use of brain cells.

She shook her head. "If it's a word, I've never heard it."

"It's not a word!" he blurted. "It's *part* of a word. The Machine shorted out before it was finished." He spun around and played the clip again. But when he looked back to Jen and me, he saw we were still clueless.

"*Hosanna!*" He practically yelled. "They were shouting *Hosanna!*"

Jen and I both nodded, giving him a polite little smile. Which, apparently, was not enough.

"Don't you get it?" He reached for a Bible on the table and started flipping the pages.

"Yeah, sure, Dad," I said, trying to calm him down. "The Machine recorded some crowd in the Bible days, waving branches and shouting—"

He interrupted and began reading:

The next day a great multitude that had come to the feast, when they heard that Jesus was coming to Jerusalem, took branches of palm trees and went out to meet Him, and cried out: "Hosanna! Blessed is He who comes in the name of the Lord! The King of Israel!"

I stared back up at the screen, not believing what I'd just heard.

When Jen spoke, her voice was kinda small and quiet. "You mean . . ." She swallowed and tried again. "You think . . ."

It was my turn. "They were shouting to Jesus?"

Dad slowly closed the Bible and looked back at the screen. "That's Palm Sunday up there, kids. We're seeing the day Jesus rode into Jerusalem on a donkey . . . five days before they crucified Him on the cross and one week before He rose from the dead."

Chapter Seventeen

THE PLOT SICKENS

J
A
K
E

It was sometime around noon when they had me hauling the snooty woman's luggage back up the hill to the helicopter pad. No one was happy to see her go. Especially Gita.

"But Miss Albright," Gita was saying as we trudged up the hill. "Can you not stay for just one more day?"

"I've wasted enough time here," the old lady grumbled. "Nor do I particularly enjoy nearly getting myself killed."

"But Dr. Mackenzie insists we are very close to success."

"And I'll be very happy to read about that success in the news . . . from some place very safe and very far away."

The three of us continued walking to the helicopter, which was already warming up. Well, the two of them were walking. I was staggering, stumbling, and dragging myself up the hill behind them. Who knew how one person could have so much junk? Then I remembered all of Jen's suitcases (which, by the way, still hadn't arrived) and realized Miss Albright was just a rookie.

The helicopter blades worked up quite a wind and Gita had to fight to keep her headscarf from flying away. "Surely you understand what happened yesterday was an act of sabotage."

"I understand that's what Dr. Mackenzie claims," Miss Albright said.

"You do not believe him?"

"I believe he needs my money to continue this operation. And I believe he will say whatever it takes to get it."

By now we were so close to the helicopter that Gita was shouting to be heard. "But without your help, the world will never know what truths the Machine can reveal."

"Maybe. Or maybe someone else will reveal them."

Gita frowned.

Miss Albright continued, "Do you honestly think you're the only people pursuing this technology?"

Gita's frown deepened.

If Miss Albright answered, you couldn't tell; not over the

thump-thump-thump

of the helicopter blades. And the

gasp-gasp-gasp

of the luggage-carrier.

When we finally arrived, Gita slid open the helicopter door and we saw . . .

"Hi there!" It was Hazel, Robbie's wannabe girlfriend sitting in the pilot's seat . . . and of course Monkey Boy sitting in the copilot's seat beside her.

"You're the pilot?" Miss Albright looked majorly concerned.

"You betcha." Hazel flashed her way-too-cheery grin. "Hop in." The chimp looked over his shoulder and smiled back at the woman.

Miss Albright hesitated.

"Don't worry," Hazel shouted, "I'm a great pilot. I've had my license for nearly a month, which is a lot longer than the last two times they took it away."

Somehow this didn't help.

Monkey Boy raised his eyebrows up and down at the woman.

That didn't help, either.

Gita glanced at her watch. "Miss Albright, if you are leaving, you must hurry to catch your flight."

With a deep breath of reluctance, Miss Money Bags finally climbed on board the helicopter while I dumped all her bags into the back luggage compartment.

"I am sorry for the way things turned out!" Gita shouted over the pounding blades. "I hope you will come again!"

The woman totally ignored her.

Sadly, Gita slid the door shut, but not before I noticed something kinda strange: not only was Monkey Boy still smiling and raising his eyebrows at the woman . . . but now he was winking.

We stepped back and ducked our heads from the flying sand as the helicopter began to rise from the pad and head for the airport. At least that's where we thought it was heading.

But we'd barely turned and started down the hill before the sound of the engine changed. We turned to see it was coming back down, fast and

SLAM!

hard.

It barely hit the ground before the door slid open and Miss Albright leaped out, screaming, "GET HIM OFF ME! GET HIM OFF ME!" (Which is just the thing to scream when a chimpanzee is riding on top of your shoulders).

"GET HIM OFF! GET HIM OFF!"

"Hang on!" Gita shouted as we raced back up the hill. "Do not panic!"

But it was kinda hard not to panic. The chimpanzee wasn't just riding her shoulders. To keep things interesting, he was also clawing at . . .

"MY HAIR!" she shouted. "HE'S EATING MY HAIR!"

By now, Hazel had jumped out of her side of the chopper and raced around to help. "He's not eating it!" she shouted. "He's smelling it! Maximilian loves the smell of hair spray. Don't worry!"

But Miss Albright WAS worrying, big time. And she was also panicking, even BIGGER TIME, which explains . . .

— why she was stumbling,
— why Maximilian was hanging on for his life,
— why he was wrapping his little arms around her head and
— why his little hands were accidentally covering her eyes.

It would also explain why, in the middle of all the shouting, screaming, and stumbling, Miss Albright lost her balance, fell to the ground and began

ROLL,
    ROLL,
        ROLLING . . .

down the hill.

"MISS ALBRIGHT!" the girls shouted.

The good news was the hill wasn't too steep (unless you're carrying luggage up it).

The bad news was the very big power pole down at the bottom. The very big power pole made out of very hard steel. The very big power pole made out of very hard steel that was *not* the type of thing you'd want to hit while

ROLL,
    ROLL,
        ROLLING . . .

down a hill—particularly with a chimp sitting on your shoulders and smelling your—

THUD!

Well, he had been smelling her hair. But when she slammed into the power pole and stopped, Monkey Boy did not. Unfortunately, neither did her hair. She hit the pole so hard that both the chimp and her wig went flying.

That's right . . . her WIG.

Suddenly, Miss Snooty was as bald as a billiard ball. She scrambled back to her feet and screamed for all she was worth (which, remember, is a lot). "My hair, my hair!" (Though, technically, it should have been, "My wig, my wig!")

Meanwhile, Hazel began chasing her pesky pet and his new possession. "Maximilian! Sweetie!"

But Maximilian Sweetie had run off to parts unknown, lost in hair spray heaven, while Miss Albright was . . . well, not exactly in heaven.

"Oh, you wretched people!" she screamed. "Wretched, wretched, wretched!"

Gita took off her scarf and immediately covered the sobbing woman's head. But it didn't help. After a little more hysterical screaming, Miss Megabucks pulled herself together, adjusted her clothing and took out her ultra-expensive smart phone . . . which was ultra-expensively shattered.

Angrily, she threw it to the ground and yelled at Gita, "Give me your phone!"

Gita pulled hers out and handed it to the woman. "Who may I ask are you calling?"

"Someone who can ensure I arrive safely at the airport." The old lady raised her nose high into the air. "Someone far more competent than you people!"

Gita frowned. "And who is that?"

"Maria Johnson."

Gita's jaw dropped. "Dr. Maria Johnson, our competition?"

"As you know, she's working on a project similar to yours." The woman finished dialing and put the phone to her ear. "Perhaps she is the one who should have my money!"

Chapter Eighteen

FAMILY FEUD

J
E
N
N
I
F
E
R

"Come on, Jen." Jake was practically dragging me toward the central lab tent.

"What's the big deal?" I grumbled.

"Dad is incredibly bummed about Miss Albright leaving. I thought maybe we could cheer him up."

I gave him a look. "Since when has Jake Mackenzie cared for anybody but Jake Mackenzie?"

He paused a moment, then shrugged. "Good point. Still, he is our dad."

I wanted to fire off something mean like, *What do we care what he feels?* Or *I'm glad he's feeling rejected; give him a taste of his own medicine.* But, of course, that's way too immature to say. Think, yes, but not say. Besides, I figured immature was more Jake's department.

Then, out of the blue, he said, "Hey, do you remember the time he came home and surprised Mom on their anniversary?"

"On what he *thought* was their anniversary," I said.

"He only missed it by a week, that's pretty good for Dad.

I nodded. He was right about that.

"And remember how mad she got because she was in her sweats and her hair was all weird and dirty."

I smiled at the memory.

"Women." Jake shook his head. "The guy travels half way around the world to surprise her and the first thing she does is yell at him."

I shrugged. "Mom could get pretty worked up."

"Yeah," he answered softly. A long moment passed before he added, "They really loved each other, didn't they."

I nodded. "With all their hearts."

We walked in more silence as I started thinking of other good times we'd had together. Little things like the four of us camping in the backyard . . . when it started raining. Or Mom dragging us to all those museums, and Dad making stupid poses and faces to keep us amused. Or Dad trying to fix breakfast Christmas morning and how grateful we were for Mom driving us to a nearby Denny's Restaurant.

After a minute or so Jake interrupted my thoughts. "Do you miss her?"

I answered quietly. "Every day."

"Me too." His voice grew thicker. "Me too."

As we continued across camp, I wondered why everything was so still, where everybody had gone . . . until we arrived at the lab and stepped through the doorway.

Seriously, it was like half the team was there—Dad, Robbie, Hazel (complete with Maximilian), Samuel the Frenchman with the beret, Hector, a crew member from South America, Ibrahim, who was the Arab with the cool robe and headdress, and Isaac, the big Jewish man who hated Ibrahim almost as much as Ibrahim hated him. Gita had just returned from dropping off Miss Albright at Jesse's mom's camp so she was there too. Everyone was gathered around something on the floor that we couldn't make out because they blocked it.

"Now, Robbie," Dad was saying as we entered, "you're sure you've got all the bugs worked out this time?" It seemed to be his standard Robbie question.

To which Robbie gave his standard Robbie answer: "Of course, it's all good. Everything's ready."

Jake and I traded uneasy looks.

But what really made us uneasy was when we worked our way through the crowd and saw the small, glowing triangle platform. It rose a couple inches above the ground and was big enough for a man to stand on. There were little lights all around the edges that were pulsating.

"What's going on?" Jake asked.

Of course he expected the entire group to stop what they were doing and answer him (since he still thought the entire world revolved around him), but everyone was too busy thinking and talking among themselves. Well, everybody but Hazel, who spotted us.

"Oh, hi there," she chirped in that ever-cheery voice of hers. "I hear you two are having a *fantastic* time."

I tried not to roll my eyes. Her idea of fantastic was definitely different from mine.

"So, what's going on?" Jake asked again.

Hazel answered, "Dr. Robbie is firing up the dimensional folder."

I felt myself growing cold. "The dimensional folder?" I croaked.

Jake turned to me, thinking he had to explain. "That's the thing Dad used to visit us back in California."

Thank you, Mr. Einstein, I thought.

He continued, "I hope it's working better than the last time."

"So do we." Hazel grinned.

I glanced over at Gita. I could tell by the look on her face that she knew exactly what I was thinking: *This was the very machine that was somehow connected to the creepy shadow thing I'd been seeing.*

"Here you go." Robbie handed Isaac what looked like a miniature hearing aide. "Just slip this in your ear and we'll be able to communicate." He nodded to the French man. Samuel, here, will be tracking you by satellite on the big screen."

Isaac nodded and put the communicator in his ear. Meanwhile, I moved across the room to join Gita. She smiled and gave my arm a quiet squeeze. Something that said, *I'm right here with you, you'll be okay.*

"And you're sure everything is safe?" Isaac was asking.

"Perfectly," Robbie said. "If our microchip is in the Johnson camp, we'll definitely find it."

As they spoke, I leaned over to Gita and whispered. "What are they doing?"

She explained, "They are preparing to transport Isaac into Maria Johnson's compound so that he might retrieve the circuit her group has stolen."

I motioned to the dimensional folder. "And they're using that?"

"The Johnson compound is heavily guarded. The only way to get past their security and to the main office is to dimensionalize directly into it."

"Did you tell them . . ." I swallowed and tried again. "Did you tell them what I've been seeing? Did you tell them about the shadow thing?"

She shook her head.

"Why not?"

"It is doubtful they would understand."

I nodded, not exactly thrilled.

"However, the use of the dimensional folder may attract the entity's attention, so you and I must be on guard."

I nodded, even less thrilled. Glancing around the room, I looked for any signs of moving shadows . . . particularly the giant, winged type.

"All right." Robbie was talking to Isaac. "Any more questions?"

The big man shook his head.

Robbie moved over to the large glowing table in the center of the room and started typing on one of the computer terminals. There was a slight hum from the triangle platform as the lights around it began to pulse faster. He motioned to Isaac. "Take your position, please."

"With great pleasure," Isaac said as he stepped onto the platform. Turning, he looked straight at Ibrahim and continued, "It is time to make right what others have tried to destroy."

Ibrahim bristled. "Are you speaking of me?"

Isaac held his look. "Who else?"

Grabbing his robe, Ibrahim started toward the platform, until Hector took his arm to hold him back.

But Isaac wasn't finished. "Who else would have anything to gain from helping others steal our hard work?"

"Gain?" Ibrahim demanded. "What would I have to gain?"

"Gentlemen," Dad raised his hands. "Please, this is no time to argue."

But Ibrahim was pretty worked up. He shook off Hector and took a step closer to Isaac. "All I hear are accusations from this man. Rumors and accusations. The microchip was clearly stolen by another and yet you continue to soil my reputation! Why? Why would I want to ruin such a great project as this?"

"You are Arab, are you not?"

"And what does that mean?"

Isaac merely smirked.

The hum of the platform grew louder, the lights pulsed faster.

"Are you saying we are not interested in history's

truth?" Ibrahim was so angry his voice trembled. "Are you saying Arabs are evil and do not care for what is true?"

"Stand by!" Robbie shouted over the hum of the platform.

Still holding Ibrahim's gaze, Isaac raised his head and folded his arms. "I am saying you are liars, thieves, and none of you are to be trusted!"

Ibrahim could stand no more. He leaped onto the platform at Isaac . . . just as the machine gave a loud

SIZZLE

followed by a blinding FLASH of light.

Suddenly Isaac was gone.

Unfortunately, so was Ibrahim.

"Uh-oh," Robbie said.

"Uh-oh, what?" Dad asked, looking around. "What happened to Ibrahim?"

"Uh-oh," Robbie repeated as he hit a few keystrokes on the computer and motioned to the big screen behind us.

That's when everyone turned and realized that "uh-oh" might be a huge understatement.

Chapter Nineteen

ROBBIE ~~STRIKES~~ HELPS AGAIN

J
A
K
E

Actually, it was pretty cool and way too funny . . . at least for those of us watching the screen. Well, maybe not for all of us. Well, okay, maybe just for me. But, I mean, picture it: two guys who hate each other have suddenly gotten plopped together right in the middle of our enemy's compound.

Not only that, but . . .

They got plopped on top of a steep roof where, if anyone from the compound looked up, they could easily be seen.

But here's the best (or worst) part . . .

The dimensional folder still wasn't working right.

The good news is it was working better than before, I mean everybody had normal looking bodies.

But the bad news was, those normal-looking bodies only wore one set of clothes.

That's right. Even though their bodies were completely intact, they were crammed together, back to back, inside Ibrahim's robe, which had grown a bunch of sizes too big.

"Robbie!" Isaac shouted.

"Shh, they'll hear you," Ibrahim whispered as he scanned the compound below them. But, when he noticed what they had to share, he cried, even louder than Isaac, "ROBBIE!"

"Sorry about that," Robbie spoke into an overhead microphone. "Guess we got a few glitches to work out."

Isaac's earpiece was close enough to Ibrahim's head so he could hear. "A few?" he growled. "This man is wearing my clothes."

"Tell me about it," Isaac growled back. Then, acting like Ibrahim was way too dirty to touch, Isaac started to slip out of the robe, until . . .

"Oops," he said.

"Oops what?" Ibrahim asked.

Isaac motioned under their robe. "All I have on is my underwear."

"That is no concern of mine," Ibrahim said. "Now, please, remove yourself from my clothes."

"Guys," Dad said.

"What if I said this robe was *my* robe," Isaac argued. "What would you do about that?"

"This can't possibly be your robe!"

"It can't possibly be yours. It's the size of a tent."

"Guys!"

"It is more my robe than yours."

"Says who?"

"Says me!"

"GUYS!"

The two men came to a stop.

Dad continued talking patiently to the screen. "It doesn't matter whose robe it is, the two of you are going to have to wear it and work together."

"I'm not working with him," Isaac said.

Ibrahim replied, "And I most certainly am not working with you."

Ignoring them, Dad said, "First we have to get you off that roof."

Isaac nodded. "Correct." He turned and started to his left.

"Wait one moment," Ibrahim said and began pulling the opposite direction. "I wish to go to the right."

"Guys." Dad looked to Robbie, who was frantically working the keyboard.

Ibrahim argued, "As long as we are wearing my clothes, we shall do as I say."

"Who says these are your clothes?"

"Guys!"

"I say!" Ibrahim gave a tug.

"Well, I don't!" Isaac tugged the opposite direction.

"Well, I do." Ibrahim tugged back. Before you knew it, it turned into a tug of war, each man pulling the opposite direction.

"This way!"

"No, this way!"

But, all good things must come to an end. Before we knew it, Isaac's foot slipped on the steep roof and they started tumbling down. "We're falling!" he cried.

"But I do not wish to fall your way. I wish to fall mine!"

Of course they were already in motion and since Isaac outweighed Ibrahim by a good hundred pounds, they

roll,
      roll,
            rolled

and

fell,
      fell,
          fe—

THUD!

The good news was nobody got hurt because they landed someplace nice and soft.

The bad news was it was nice and soft because it was inside a camel pen.

The worst news was it was a camel pen with plenty of camel poop.

Ibrahim groaned. "What is that awful smell?"

Isaac sniffed. "When's the last time you showered?"

"Everybody okay?" Dad asked.

"Yeah," Isaac said. Both men staggered to their feet, only to discover they were knee deep in camel manure.

"Your robe is filthy," Isaac said.

"Who says it is my robe?"

"You did."

"You said it was yours."

They continued bickering as Robbie frantically typed in code, trying to fix the problem.

"Samuel," Dad called to the French guy working at another terminal, "pull back and let's see how far we are from the main office."

Samuel typed a few keystrokes and the picture on the screen zoomed out so we could see a large tent a couple buildings from the men. It was flashing red.

"Okay gentlemen," Dad said. "It looks like there are two buildings between you and the target."

"I thought as much," Isaac said. "So we'll turn right and head around this building." He started pulling Ibrahim with him.

But of course, Ibrahim had other ideas. "I believe we must go to the left."

"Guys," Dad said, "you can't keep fighting like this. You have to work together."

"I am working together, you must make him work together."

"I'm the one working together, you're the problem."

And around and around they went until Dad saw something and shouted, "Two men approaching from your left at ten o'clock. Take cover!"

"This way!" Isaac said, pulling them around the corner.

"No, this way!" Ibrahim yelled.

"Hurry!" Dad shouted. "They're almost there!"

"As long as you wear my clothes we will go—"

"You said they were my clothes!"

"All right!" Robbie shouted from across the table. "I've got it."

Dad turned to him. "You fixed it?"

"Of course!"

"Well, hurry!"

"Take it easy boss," Robbie said. "It's all under control." To make his point, he raised his hand high above his head, stuck out a finger, and brought it down onto the keyboard.

There was another blinding FLASH. We all turned to the screen. Dad was the first to see it and groaned, "Oh, no."

Isaac and Ibrahim were the second:

"ROBBIE!"

Chapter Twenty

A CHANGE IN WARDROBE

J
A
K
E

The good news was Isaac and Ibrahim no longer wore Ibrahim's giant, manure-covered robe.

The bad news was they now wore Isaac's T-shirt, which had grown ten sizes too big along with his newly enlarged pair of jeans.

And, of course, the worst news was they were still facing opposite directions.

"Well," Isaac sighed, "I suppose this is a little better."

Ibrahim glanced inside their clothes and replied, "Not really."

"Why's that?" Isaac asked.

"We are still wearing only our underwear."

"Don't worry fellas," Robbie said, as his fingers flew over the keyboard, "I'm working on it."

It was Ibrahim's turn to sigh. "That is what I am afraid of."

"You're not out of trouble, yet," Dad said. "Those two men are still approaching. Do you see that corner of the building to your right? Run around it and hide against the wall."

Both men started to argue until Dad cut them off. "Do it!"

So began one of the funniest races in history . . . as the men ran, tripped, and stumbled, bickering all the way:

"Move your left leg with my right leg."

"No, move your right leg with my left leg."

Finally they made it around the corner and pressed themselves against the wall. But even then the bickering wasn't over.

"*Shh,*" Isaac said.

"Do not tell me to *shh,*" Ibrahim said. "You *shh.*"

"I am *shh*ing."

"You're not *shh*ing, you're talking."

"I'm not talking as much as you're—"

"Gentlemen," Dad shouted. "Zip it!"

That seemed to do the trick.

All of us in the lab held our breath as the two men from the compound walked past without even looking over their shoulders.

Once they were gone, Dad leaned into his mic and calmly spoke. "It looks like they're heading for the main office. Let them get a good twenty yards ahead and then follow them . . . *silently.*"

Isaac and Ibrahim nodded and waited. Meanwhile, Robbie wildly typed away. I glanced over to Jen. Odd, but for some reason she wasn't there. During all the action she must have slipped out.

"Okay, guys," Dad spoke into the mic again. "Let's get started." Before they could argue, he continued, "On my count. First Isaac, you'll move your left leg and Ibrahim, your right. Got it?"

They nodded.

He began. "And . . . one."

They did as he said.

"Now your opposite legs. Two."

They did.

Dad continued counting. "One . . . two. One . . . two," as the guys began making progress. It was interesting to see the way he took charge, how everyone respected him. It made me think how many times we could have used someone like that to take charge around the house. Not that Mom didn't try but, you know, Mom was, well, Mom. And watching him lead all these people and take control here, when he could have been doing it at home . . . well, it didn't exactly make me mad, like it did Jen. It just made me kind of sad.

"Samuel," Dad called across the table, "Switch to infrared. Let's see what's going on inside that main office."

Samuel typed in some keystrokes and the picture on the screen turned all green and white, like with night vision goggles. Now we could see inside the office, where a dozen white blobs shaped like humans were sitting in chairs facing another white blob.

"Hector," Dad called. "Bring up the audio. Let's hear what he's saying."

Hector moved to another keyboard on the lighted table and started typing.

"Okay, guys," Dad spoke into the mic again. "You see that open window to your right? I want you to get as close to it as you can. *And no talking.* We're turning your microphone up to maximum volume so we can hear what's being said inside."

Isaac and Ibrahim nodded and quietly crept to the open window.

— The good news was the people inside were in the middle of an important meeting.
— The bad news was they were saying lots of boring junk.
— The good news is I'll spare you the boring junk.
— The bad news is when we finally got to the good news, it wasn't exactly good.

One of the white blobs was talking. "Are you saying we went to all the effort of stealing that circuit from Mackenzie's camp and now you've lost it?"

Another blob answered. "Well, I wouldn't exactly call it lost."

I couldn't be sure, but that second blob sounded like the same guy whose Jeep Robbie's gyromower crashed into.

"Well, what exactly would you call it?"

"More like . . . temporarily misplaced."

The people in the room groaned quietly.

Unfortunately, Ibrahim sighed softly. And with the microphone turned up all the way, softly was more like LOUDLY!

Unfortunately, LOUDLY! meant feedback through Isaac's ear piece.

Unfortunatelier (is that a word?) the feedback

SQUEALED

even LOUDLIER! (now I *know* that's not a word) in Isaac's ear until he shouted "YEOW!" in pain.

"What was that?" the first blob asked.

"It came from the window," the second said as he moved toward it

Dad was immediately on the mic whispering to Isaac, "They're coming toward you! Drop down and stay out of sight."

They did just that as the first blob arrived at the window a couple feet above them.

"Don't say a word," Dad whispered.

"Okay," Isaac whispered . . . but with the microphone turned up, it sounded more like OKAY . . . which blasted through his earpiece leading to an even louder

SQUEAL

leading to an even louder "YEOW!"

The blob stuck his head out the window and looked down at them.

Isaac looked up and smiled. *"Shalom,"* he said (whatever that means).

Ibrahim looked up and also smiled. *"As-salam alay-kum,"* he said (whatever that means).

"SPIES!" the blob shouted. (We all know what that means.)

Isaac was the first to take off running. Of course it would have been better if he had warned his partner, since they were still sharing the same clothes. But little details like that can be hard to remember when you're running for your life. Well, in Isaac and Ibrahim's case, running, stumbling, and falling for their lives.

One of the first people out of the room was old money-bags herself—Miss Albright. "What are you doing here?" she shouted after them. But the guys were too busy stumbling and falling to answer.

Since they spent half their time on the ground, it was easy for the others to catch up and surround them. And since Miss Albright was the maddest, she got into their faces the soonest. "Were you sent here to spy on me?"

"Stand by to dimensionalize!" Robbie shouted. "On my count. Three . . ."

"Answer me!" Miss Albright yelled.

"Two . . ."

"Any time," Ibrahim whispered.

"Why are you here!"

"One . . ."

"Now would be good," Isaac agreed.

There was another blinding FLASH!

And there, standing on the dimensional folder's platform, inside *our* tent was . . . Miss Albright! To make matters worse her skirt and blouse were replaced by Isaac's T-shirt and jeans.

"Robbie!" we all yelled.

To make matters worse than that worse, Isaac and Ibrahim were still in the other camp, wearing only their underwear.

"ROBBIE!"

"I'm on it!" he shouted. "I'm on it!"

Meanwhile, the crowd surrounding Isaac and Ibrahim started closing in.

"What do we do?" Isaac yelled. "What do we do?"

Dad leaned into his mic. "I'm no expert, but maybe—"

"Maybe what?" they cried.

"RUN!"

It seemed to make sense so they took off.

"Stand by," Robbie shouted.

"We're ready!" the two men yelled.

Robbie hit a final key and FLASH! the crowd was gone.

Well, not exactly gone. Now *they* were all standing in the lab tent staring at us.

"ROBBIE!"

He hit another key and there was another FLASH!

The good news was they were no longer in the lab tent.

The bad news was *we* were all in *their* camp.

"ROBB—"

FLASH!

And finally, *finally*, everybody was where they belonged—Ibrahim, Isaac, everybody from our team, everybody from their team, even Miss Albright. Everybody was exactly where they should be.

Well, everybody but the camp's camel, who stood in our tent . . . wearing Miss Albright's skirt and blouse.

Chapter Twenty-One

DÉJÀ VU ALL OVER AGAIN

J
E
N
N
I
F
E
R

While everybody else was having fun, I was having a slightly different experience. As soon as Isaac and Ibrahim cross-dimensionalized to the other camp, I spotted movement in the shadows of the lab tent—under the tables, behind the chairs, off in the corners. At first I thought my eyes were playing tricks on me, because whenever I looked right at the shadows, I saw nothing. But when I glanced to the side, I could see them moving out of the corner of my eye.

And that was freaky.

It was like they were quivering . . . drifting toward each other. That's when I figured it was time to step outside and get a breath of fresh air.

As I started to leave, Gita looked over to me and whispered, "Is there something wrong?"

I shook my head. It was probably just my imagination and I didn't need to embarrass myself in front of her any more. I stepped outside and shut the door behind me. I took about a dozen steps and looked back over my shoulder . . . just in time to see the shadows had combined and were slithering under the door, moving across the ground . . . straight for me.

This can't be happening! I thought. *I'm wide awake!*

But it *was* happening. And the faster I walked, the faster they came, until I finally broke into a run. That's when I heard it—over the noise from the tent, over the wind blowing against my ears, over my own breathing. It was like the clicking, clucking sound that crows make when they chortle. And it was getting louder by the second.

Closer by the second.

I darted around the next tent and started running full tilt. That's when I heard another sound . . . like a sheet snapping in the wind. It happened a second time, slow and deliberate. I knew I shouldn't look, but I had to. I turned and saw the shadow had formed wings and was flapping them. It was rising off the ground!

I spotted another tent to my right, a work area almost as big as the lab tent. I raced to it and ducked through the open door. I glanced back as the thing pulled in its wings to enter and again flew toward me. I ran past one cluttered worktable and then another. I could hear it closing in as it clicked and cackled, its wings knocking beakers and things off the table. Suddenly, I realized I was at a dead end—there was no way out but back through the door I'd just entered.

I veered to the left around a table. But the thing flew across the table to cut me off . . . until I darted to the right and doubled back for the door. That's when I got a close look at it. We were just a few feet apart and I saw the outline of a beak and, even though it was only shadow, I saw my own reflection in its shiny red eye.

With a surge of adrenalin, I raced for the open door, thirty feet away. The thing let out a shriek of anger as it turned after me.

The door was twenty feet from me.

I heard it flap its wings.

Fifteen feet ahead . . . ten feet.

I heard it breathing now—ragged, raspy gasps. It gave its wings another flap.

Five feet.

I felt it touch my shoulder. I yanked away and shot through the door. This time I slammed it shut behind me. There was a muffled thud, more like a puff of wind. I looked back and saw I'd stopped it . . . for a moment. But I wouldn't slow down. I had to get back to the lab tent. I had to get to Gita. My lungs ached for air but I kept running.

I heard the clicking and clucking again. I glanced over my shoulder to see the shadow had broken apart into little ones. They were all shapes and sizes as they slipped under the door, then they quickly pulled back together again.

I ran harder. My legs started to feel like rubber. But I didn't stop and I didn't look back. I didn't have to. I heard the wings flap . . . and then again. It was airborne.

My lungs burned. My legs were losing feeling but still I ran, pushing as hard as I could. I saw the lab tent just ahead. The sound of the wings rose above me. I stumbled, but kept running. The clucking was directly over my head now. I didn't look up. I didn't have to. That's when my right leg twisted. It was like part of me watching a slow-motion movie as I lost my balance and fell forward. For a moment I almost caught myself.

Almost.

I hit the ground, knees and elbows digging into the sand. I rolled onto my back. And there, right above me, floated the shadowy outline, its claws just a couple feet away. I opened my mouth to scream, but no sound came. It was like one of those nightmares where you can't move, you can't even shout.

But this was no nightmare.

The thing opened its beak, clicking and clacking. I tried to turn, but I was frozen in fear. It lowered its head, my reflection growing bigger in those red eyes. Somewhere in the back of my mind, I remember thinking, *Jesus . . . help me!* If it was a prayer, it wasn't much. But it must have been something, because the shadow paused. It tilted its head and then—

"Jennifer, what is wrong?"

I turned to see Gita running out of the lab tent towards me.

"What has happened? Are you injured?"

I tried to answer. "I . . . it . . ."

"Is it here?" She kneeled down just below the thing. It wavered and shifted to the side, like it was afraid she would touch it. "The creature from your dreams? Is it here?"

My eyes darted from her to the shadow, then back to her.

"Jennifer. Is it here?"

Somehow I managed a nod.

Gita turned, searching for it. It was three feet away but she couldn't see it.

"You did not order it to leave? You did not use your authority?"

"I . . ." I shook my head.

She frowned and slowly rose to her feet. The shadow pulled back farther. And then she spoke—loud and with total authority. "Whoever you are, whatever you are . . . I order you to leave!"

The shadow opened its beak and hissed directly into her face. But Gita didn't notice. If she did, she didn't care. "You have heard me. By the power and authority of Jesus Christ, I order you to go."

The shadow rippled. It raised its wings and glowered at her. But she wouldn't back down.

"Now!" she demanded. "I command you to go, now!"

The rippling grew faster, more violent. It threw back its head. A cry began somewhere deep in its throat. It grew into a scream, louder and louder as it began to twist and squirm . . . and then dissolve.

"Now!" Gita shouted.

It shrieked.

"In Jesus's name, go now!"

The shadow exploded. I ducked as pieces flew in all directions, until they faded and completely disappeared. The shriek took longer to fade, but then it was also gone.

Finally Gita looked down at me. "Has he . . . has it left?

I nodded.

She knelt beside me and gently pushed the sweaty hair out of my face. "You are shaking," she said.

I tried to answer but could only nod.

"Why did you not use your authority?"

"I don't . . . I . . ."

"Are you not a Christian?"

I shrugged. "Not a very good one."

"But you are forgiven and you have the authority." Quietly she quoted, "'I give you the authority to trample on serpents and scorpions and over all the power of the enemy.' These are Jesus' words, Jennifer, not mine."

I nodded.

"We may fail Him, but He will never fail us."

I closed my eyes as she continued. "As the daughter of God Almighty, you have that authority. All you must do is trust Him and use it."

Chapter Twenty-Two

LESSONS REVISITED

J
E
N
N
I
F
E
R

An hour later we were sitting outside Gita's tent, sipping tea. Once again it was like the night sky was showing off with a million stars all blazing down on us. Even though the shadow thing was long gone, it was good to be with her. I felt safe. And, as always, she somehow managed to get me to say what was really on my mind.

"I don't know why it always has to be me," I grumbled.

"I do not understand," she said.

"I'm the one whose mother died. I'm the one whose father barely knows her from Adam or Eve. I'm the one who keeps seeing this . . . thing. I mean if God loves me so much, why does all this stuff keep happening to me?"

Gita took a long sip of tea. After what seemed forever, she spoke. "I have learned a long time ago never to question God."

I turned to her, waiting for more.

She pointed to an ant moving across the arm of her chair. "It would be like this ant questioning what we are doing. Even if I explained it to him, he would not understand."

I took a drink of tea.

She continued. "The Bible tells us that God's ways are not our ways. We can no more figure out what He is doing, than this ant can understand what I am doing."

I sighed in agreement. "Tell me about it."

"But the Bible also says His ways are *better* than ours . . . even when they do not make sense."

I said nothing. I mean, how are you supposed to argue with the Bible?

She continued, "When I was a little girl, the very first verse I memorized was from Romans 8:28. Do you know it?"

I shook my head.

She quoted, "'All things work together for good to those who love God, to those who are the called according to His purpose.'" She continued. "Not *some* things, Jennifer. Not *most* things. But *ALL* things."

And you believe that?" I asked.

"I have seen it. In my life over and over again I have seen this to be true. Not always, immediately—but always, eventually. If you love God, everything will work together for your good—this creature, your father's neglect, even your mother's death."

I bristled. "Are you telling me there's *nothing* bad?"

"No, there is much evil in the world. But He promises to take that evil and turn it around for your good."

I bit my lip, feeling my eyes fill with moisture as I thought about Mom . . . about Dad . . . about everything.

Gita must have seen it, because she lowered her voice and continued more gently. "No, my friend. I no longer ask God why. That is questioning His wisdom, His authority. But there is something I do ask Him."

I turned to her and waited.

"I ask him . . . how."

"How?"

She nodded. "*How* can I use these difficulties, *how* can I use these tragedies?"

"Why, how?" I shrugged. "I don't see the difference."

"*Why* says I don't trust You. It questions His authority. But *how* says I trust You—show me *how* I can use it to accomplish Your purposes, *how* I can join forces with what You are doing to accomplish good."

That was a brain full and I wasn't sure I bought it. But instead of arguing, I looked back up to the stars.

"Beautiful, aren't they?" she asked.

"Yes." I gave my eyes a quick swipe. "There are so many lights in Los Angeles, we never see anything like this."

She nodded, then she pointed, "Do you see that bright band above us, running all the way down to the horizon?"

I nodded.

"That is our galaxy; the Milky Way."

"I thought galaxies were flat and spirally."

"We are looking at its edge. Seeing a side view.

I nodded. "How many stars do you think are in it?"

"Spiral galaxies average about a hundred billion stars apiece."

I shook my head, trying to wrap my mind around that number.

As if reading my thoughts, she said, "That's roughly twenty-five thousand times the amount of people living in Los Angeles. And that's just one galaxy."

"How many are there in the universe? Galaxies, I mean."

"Between a hundred to five hundred billion."

I blinked. My mind was definitely on overload.

"Which brings the total number of stars to . . ." Gita paused until I turned and saw her smiling at me mischievously.

"Okay," I said, bracing myself. "I'm ready."

"It is estimated there are up to fifty trillion stars in the universe."

I whistled quietly and looked back up.

"Do you think the God who created all of these stars is not powerful enough to use even the bad for your good?"

I glanced down.

"He loved you more than His own life, Jennifer. That is why He died on the cross."

I swallowed back the lump growing in my throat and gave my eyes another swipe.

"He knows what you are going through and, believe me, He feels every ounce of your pain. He will use it for your good . . . that is what He has promised. I did not make that promise. Nor did your father. But the very God who created all of these stars made that promise. *All things work together for the good*, my friend. Not some things, not most things, but *all* things."

She took another sip of tea and quietly repeated what she'd said just an hour earlier. "You must simply put your trust in Him."

I had nothing to say—which was a good thing, because Jake suddenly came running up to us. "Guys!" he shouted. "Robbie wants everybody in the lab tent, pronto."

A look of concern crossed Gita's face as she rose to her feet. "Is there a problem?"

"Not unless you call getting the Machine up and running a problem. Let's go! You, too, Jen. Everybody's gotta pitch in if this is going to happen!"

Chapter Twenty-Three

A STICKY SITUATION

J
A
K
E

It was cool the way everybody pitched in together on the Machine. Robbie was pretty sure if we worked through the night we could make a circuit board to replace the one that got stolen. It would be a million times bigger since it would be built out of clunkier stuff and we didn't have the ability to shrink it down into one of those tiny microchips, but we could still create something pretty close.

Well, *they* could still create something pretty close. Unfortunately, Jen and I had a slightly different assignment . . .

"Pick up the garbage around camp?" Jen whined.

"Not all of it," I said. "Robbie just wants the stuff picked up where that Albright chick might see."

"She's coming back?"

"If she doesn't, it's bye-bye to the Machine."

"But she's at the other camp," Jen said. "Don't they have something like the Machine over there?"

"Right. Except . . ."

"Except what?"

"They need the same microchip we need. The one your boyfriend stole."

"My boyfriend?" Jen sputtered.

(Score! Good to see I'd not lost my touch.)

"He is *not* my boyfriend!" Her ears were already starting to turn red.

"Whatever," I said. We continued toward Robbie's and my tent. "The deal is, they lost it, which means theirs won't work either, which means Albright—"

"—is going to walk out on them too?" Jen asked.

"Exactly. Robbie says she's taking the first plane back to New York tomorrow. But if we have something to show her before then—"

"She'll stay and help out Dad?"

"That's what we're hoping," I said.

We arrived at my tent and I pushed open the door. As a neat freak, I knew Jen would, well, freak. And I wasn't wrong.

"What are we doing here?" she demanded. "He doesn't expect us to clean up *this* mess!"

"Nah." I headed over to the giant mountain of junk Robbie had in the corner.

"So what are we doing?"

I began digging through the stuff. "I saw something the other day I think we can use."

"The only thing this place could use is a bulldozer . . . or some dynamite," she said.

I kept digging until I spotted it . . . the giant vacuum cleaner with all the suction hoses I'd seen when we were working on the rocket-powered gyromower (may it rest in peace).

"Here we go." I dragged it out to the middle of the tent. It was big and pretty heavy—but, thanks to my exceptional athletic ability, it wasn't a problem.

"A vacuum cleaner?" Jen asked suspiciously.

"Not just *a* vacuum cleaner," I said. I pointed to the logo on the handle that read:

NUCLEAR-POWER VACUUM CLEANER

Then I nodded to the control panel on the front that had all sorts of labeled switches. "Check it out."

She stooped down and began reading them: "*Dirt . . . Mud . . . Cat Hair . . . Leaves . . . Paper . . . Gum . . .*" She looked up at me and said, "I don't get it."

"I'm thinking each switch is for a certain type of trash. Whatever switch we flip will automatically suck up that piece of garbage."

"Automatically?" she said.

"Sure, why not?"

"Because it's a crazy idea," she said.

"Which makes it something Robbie would invent."

She looked at me and slowly nodded. "You might be right."

"Of course I'm right. The only time I was wrong was when I thought I might not be."

She totally ignored me, which I'm totally used to.

We wheeled the big machine out of the tent with all its hoses dragging behind. Outside, I bent over and began flipping the switches."

"Woah, wait a minute," she said. "Let's test it first."

"Test it?"

"Sure. Let's start with something small." She reread the categories, *"Mud . . . Cat Hair . . . Paper . . .* Oh, here's one. How does *Gum* sound?"

"*Gum?* How many pieces of gum are lying around the camp?"

"Hopefully, not many. That's what I mean about starting small."

Normally I would have argued (something I'm genetically programmed to do), but since we were pressed for time, I let it go and said, "Sure, why not."

She reached for the *Gum* switch, flipped it on, and . . . Nothing.

"Well, that was exciting," I said.

"Wait a minute. Don't we have to turn on the power or something?"

(She's such a pain when she's right.) "And how do we do that?" I asked.

"Oh, I don't know, unless it has something to do with these three buttons labeled POWER."

(See what I mean?)

"*Three* buttons?" I asked.

She nodded and pointed to the first one, which read:

Are You Sure?

Without a moment's hesitation (for which I'm incredibly famous), I reached over and pressed the button.

The giant vacuum cleaner began to HUM which, of course, meant Jen offered her usual words of encouragement. "Jake, be careful!"

Which, of course, I ignored. I reached for the next button labeled:

Are You REALLY Sure?

I pushed it and all the vacuum hoses began to glow red. Not a lot, but enough for Jen to offer more sisterly advice. "I really don't think this is a good idea!"

Which, of course, is why I reached over and pressed the third and final button. The one that read:

Okay, But Don't Say You Weren't Warned!

The HUM grew louder and the hoses glowed brighter. But, other than that, we were back to nothing happening.

Jen shouted over the noise. "Looks like it's another one of Robbie's failures."

I shook my head.

"What do you mean?"

"Robbie's inventions are never failures."

"What are they then?" she yelled.

"Catastrophes. They always work, just never in the right way."

"Well, you can see for yourself, that nothing is—"

"LOOK OUT!" I yelled. I leaped at her and tackled her to the ground in my best NFL linebacker imitation . . .

just as a giant wad of bubble gum shot across the camp and missed her by inches, as it was

SUCK-GULP-ed

through one of the hoses and into the vacuum cleaner.

When we were convinced nothing more was coming, we climbed back to our feet.

"Well, that wasn't so bad," I said.

"I don't know." Jen glanced around nervously.

"Relax. One piece of gum. It's all over."

She motioned to the vacuum cleaner. "Then why does it keep humming louder?"

She had another good point. (I hate it when that happens.)

"And why are those hoses glowing brighter?"

Another good point. (This was getting embarrassing.)

Still, I knew my required response: "The trouble with you, is you worry way too—"

"JAKE!"

I spun around just in time to see Maximilian, the chimp, flying towards us (well, actually toward the hose). He had a half-blown bubble in his mouth that he wouldn't let go of for the world (or his life) while screaming . . .

"Oo-ooo . . . Aah–aah . . . Eee-eee!"

We ducked just as he was

SUCK (but not GULPed)

onto the end of the hose. He was too big to go through and

too stubborn to let go of the gum. So he just stayed there, his mouth glued to the hose, screaming:

"Mo-mooo...Mah–maah...Mee-meee!"

which, though I don't speak Chimpeese, sounded an awful lot like, "Excuse me, but would you be so kind as to remove my face from this suction device?"

Meanwhile, the HUM had grown into a full-blown ROAR as the other hoses glowed so red they reminded me of the zit on Jen's nose at last year's All School Dance. (By the way, if this ever happens to your sister, do not, I repeat, **do not** start singing "Rudolph the Red Nose Reindeer" unless you want your mom to ground you for a month.)

Of course, being the animal lover Jen is, she began shouting, "TURN IT OFF! TURN IT OFF!"

And being the heroic type I am, I would have . . . if I wasn't distracted by Hazel running towards us, waving her arms and screaming, "WHAT HAVE YOU DONE TO SWEETIE? WHAT HAVE YOU DONE TO SWEETIE?"

"IT'S ROBBIE'S VACUUM CLEANER!" Jen shouted. "IT'S SET ON *GUM*. TELL HIM TO SPIT IT OUT! TELL HIM TO SPIT IT OUT!"

Before I could hit the power button, much less ask why everybody was repeating themselves, repeating themselves, Hazel pushed me aside and ran to the chimp, shouting, "SWEETIE, SPIT IT OUT! SPIT IT OUT!"

But of course Sweetie wouldn't spit it out, spit it out.

And then things got real crazy . . .

The HUM kept getting louder as the vacuum grew more and more powerful. First it had been one piece of gum flying in. Then one piece of gum and a monkey flying in. And now . . .

SUCK-GULP, SUCK-GULP, SUCK-GULP

lots of pieces of gum flying in from lots of different directions.

"WHERE ARE THEY COMING FROM?" I shouted, ducking and dodging as they came faster and

SUCK-GULP, SUCK-GULP, SUCK-GULP,
SUCK-GULP, SUCK-GULP, SUCK-GULP,

faster.

"IT'S SUCKING THEM FROM NEARBY VILLAGES!" Hazel yelled as she kept tugging on Maximilian. "PLEASE, SHUT IT DOWN!"

I fought my way back to the control panel, playing an impossible game of

SUCK-GULP, SUCK-GULP, SUCK-GULP,
SUCK-GULP, SUCK-GULP, SUCK-GULP,
SUCK-GULP, SUCK-GULP, SUCK-GULP,

Dodge Gum. And if that wasn't bad enough, there were a couple more bads thrown in just for fun. Little things like:

BAD THING #1:

"JAKE!" Jen shouted. "THE VACUUM BAG IS FILLING UP!"

I looked to the bag behind the machine and she was right, it was swelling up like a giant balloon.

"IT'S GOING TO EXPLODE!" she cried.

But that was nothing compared to . . .

BAD THING #2:

"JAKE!" Hazel shouted. "THERE'S A BUBBLE GUM FACTORY IN JERUSALEM!"

"SO?" I shouted.

"SO JERUSALEM IS ONLY FOUR MILES AWAY!"

"SO?"

"SO DO YOU SEE THAT GIANT CLOUD COMING AT US?"

I spun around and saw a huge cloud flying towards us. There was just enough moonlight to make out a color. "IS THAT PINK?" I shouted. "WHY IS IT PINK?"

"I'M BETTING IT'S NOT RAIN," she yelled.

"WHAT IS IT?" Jen shouted.

"OH NO!" I shouted.

"OH, YES!" Hazel yelled.

Even Maximilian got the message. Seeing it, his little chimp eyes grew big as he managed a little chimp whimper:

"Muh-moh"

But Jen, not always the brightest candle on the cake, shouted. "I DON'T GET IT! IF IT'S NOT RAIN, WHAT IS IT?"

Hazel and I both shouted: BUBBLE—

SUCK-GULP, SUCK-GULP, SUCK-GULP,
SUCK-GULP, SUCK-GULP, SUCK-GULP,
SUCK-GULP, SUCK-GULP, SUCK-GULP,
SUCK-GULP, SUCK-GULP, SUCK-GULP
SUCK-GULP, SUCK-GULP, SUCK-GULP,
SUCK-GULP, SUCK-GULP, SUCK-GULP,
SUCK-GULP, SUCK-GULP, SUCK-GULP,
SUCK-GULP, SUCK-GULP, SUCK-GULP
SUCK-GULP, SUCK-GULP, SUCK-GULP,
SUCK-GULP, SUCK-GULP, SUCK-GULP,
SUCK-GULP, SUCK-GULP, SUCK-GULP,
SUCK-GULP, SUCK-GULP, SUCK-GULP
SUCK-GULP, SUCK-GULP, SUCK-GULP,
SUCK-GULP, SUCK-GULP, SUCK-GULP,
SUCK-GULP, SUCK-GULP, SUCK-GULP,
SUCK-GULP, SUCK-GULP, SUCK-GULP

GUM!"

Unfortunately, that was the good news.

The bad news was the vacuum bag kept swelling and swelling until it couldn't handle any more and finally

BLAMB!

CHAPTER TWENTY-FOUR

ARRESTED DEVELOPMENT

J
E
N
N
I
F
E
R

"Look at you," Hazel beamed as she and I stood together staring into her full-length mirror. "We could practically be sisters."

I managed to keep my face from grimacing, though the rest of me gave a full-body shudder.

"Are you okay?" she asked.

I tried to nod. My old clothes sat in a pile, covered in

pink, sticky bubble gum. Since my suitcases still hadn't arrived, Hazel offered to let me wear some of her clothes. It's not that I didn't appreciate the offer. I mean she was sweet and kind and helpful. I just wasn't sure if white pumps, plaid knee socks, a pink chiffon skirt with ruffles all around, and a Boy Scout shirt was exactly the look I was after.

Still, beggars can't be choosers. And let's face it, I survived the bubble gum explosion better than Jake. At least I managed to duck and cover my head. Jake, on the other hand—

"So, what do you think?" Jake asked as he strolled through the open door of Hazel's tent.

I turned to see my brother sporting a new do . . . or lack-of-do. The gum had covered so much of his hair he had to shave it all off. Poor guy. He was totally bald.

"Oh, Jake . . ." I was going to tell him how sorry I was, but as usual, he was too caught up in himself to listen.

"Not bad, huh," he said running his hand over his shiny scalp.

Hazel tried to smile, but even the world's cheeriest cheerleader was having a hard time being positive.

"Pretty awesome?" Jake said, striking a pose he'd seen in some Mr. Universe magazine.

"Well," I cleared my throat, "it's pretty something."

He nodded in satisfaction. "Exactly." I waited for him to make some crack about my wardrobe, but that would mean thinking of somebody other than himself, which, of course, was impossible. Instead, he asked, "So what's the word on the Machine?"

Hazel's face lit up. "Oh, it's so incredibly exciting. Dr. Robbie radioed me just a few minutes ago and said they'll have it up and running any time now."

"Let's check it out," Jake said as he turned to the door.

"Oh, yes." Hazel clapped her hands. "Let's do, let's do."

Glancing in the mirror, I was thinking, *Let's don't, let's don't,* but I knew this was important, so I followed them out of the tent and toward the staging area. It had been a long night and the sun was just peeking up over the horizon in a beautiful sunrise.

"So," Jake asked, "what happens if you get the Machine up and running?"

Hazel answered, "We'll call Miss Albright and beg for one more chance to show her before she leaves Israel."

"When is she leaving?" I asked.

Hazel looked at her watch. "In exactly six hours, thirty-two minutes and four seconds."

"Six hours?" Jake said.

"And thirty-two minutes," I added.

"Actually, it's now six hours, thirty-one minutes and fifty-eight seconds," Hazel said. "No, make that six hours, thirty-one minutes and fifty-four seconds."

Jake and I traded looks.

"No, six hours, thirty-one minutes and fifty—"

"I get it," Jake said as we rounded the last tent and approached the staging area. "There's not much time."

"Actually six hours, thirty-one—"

"Hazel!" Dad called. "Kids! I'm glad you're here!" I threw a look to Hazel thinking, *so were we.*

The rest of the team had gathered in the open staging

area. Wires and all sorts of electronic stuff were scattered across the ground around the pedestal and clay lamp. The place looked like a Radio Shack gone berserk, which, of course, meant Hazel had to start in with the praise, "Oh, Dr. Robbie, this looks sooo . . . marvelous. You're such a genius."

But the genius didn't bother looking up. He was too busy working with one of the bigger electronic pieces lying on the ground.

When we joined Dad, I could see he was pretty tired, but also really excited. "Isn't this wonderful!" he exclaimed.

"I don't get it," Jake said.

"It looks worse than Jake's bedroom," I added.

"What you're seeing," Dad said, "is all the circuitry that's in a microchip before it's miniaturized." He held up a small microchip in his hand. "Normally, if we had the time and facilities, all of what you see on the ground would be shrunk and squeezed down into something like this."

Jake motioned to the ground. "You mean all this junk is in the microchip they stole?"

Dad nodded. "Precisely." He looked over at Robbie and called, "So how are we doing?"

"Just a few more minutes," Robbie called back. "This is the tricky part. If I can just—" He slowed to a stop, looking past us at some approaching cars.

We turned to see a dark blue Israeli police car pulling up. A black SUV was behind it.

Dad shielded his eyes against the morning sun. "What on earth?"

The doors to the police car opened and two men in uniform stepped out. Over at the SUV another man stepped out. I caught my breath. It was the roly-poly driver of the crashed Jeep.

"Dr. Philip Mackenzie," one of the officers called as they approached.

"Right here," Dad said. Then turning to the SUV driver he said, "Henderson, nice of you to come back and pay us a visit."

The officer continued, "Do you employ a Dr. Robert P. Ruttledge?"

"Yes, I do" Dad said.

"Over here," Robbie said, as he rose to his feet.

The officer looked to the SUV driver who nodded, then he turned back to Robbie and said, "I am afraid you will have to come with us."

"What?" Robbie asked as he walked over to join us. "What's this about?"

"You are under arrest."

"Arrest? What for?"

"For destroying this man's Jeep and endangering his life."

"That's absurd," Dad said. "He did no such thing." Then, turning to Robbie he asked, "Did you?"

Robbie shrugged. "It's a long story."

Dad turned back to the officers. "We're in the middle of an important scientific breakthrough here."

"We apologize for the inconvenience, Dr. Mackenzie," the first officer said. "But charges have been filed and there is a witness." He turned to Robbie. "You must come with us for questioning."

Robbie turned back to all the equipment lying on the ground.

"You don't understand," Dad said. "We are on the verge of a huge discovery. If you could wait just a few—"

"Now," the officer interrupted. "He must come with us *now*."

CHAPTER TWENTY-FIVE

FATAL BLOW

J
A
K
E

Everyone in the camp was pretty bummed about Robbie getting hauled away. But nobody took it as bad as Dad. Oh, he tried to be cool and everything, but there was something in his eyes that I hadn't seen since Mom died. Deeper than sadness. More like part of his heart had been ripped away. And I wasn't the only one who noticed. Even, Jen, no matter how mad she was at him, felt bad.

We were heading to the mess tent where he'd called a meeting when she asked, "Do you think he's going to be all right?"

"Sure," I shrugged. "You know Dad, he'll bounce back."

"I don't know," she said as we stepped through the door of the tent to join the others. "I'm not so sure."

The truth is, neither was I.

The meeting had already started so we hung toward the back as Dad continued talking. Every one of his workers was there, all two dozen of them. All two dozen men and women hoping he had some miracle up his sleeve to save the project. And every one of them was about to become very disappointed . . .

"I know we've worked long and hard on this," he was saying. "And I can't begin to tell you how much I appreciate the dedication each of you has displayed."

I glanced around the tent. It was so quiet you could hear a pin drop.

"But I'm afraid the time has finally come for me to admit I have failed you."

The group started to murmur.

He raised his hands. "I know, I know. But we have to face the facts. Our funding has dried up and there is no way I will ask you to stick around and work for free."

Samuel, the French guy, spoke up. "We will stay until you find the money."

Others agreed, but Dad shook his head. "No. I will not allow that. You all have families to feed and I will not let you put them at risk for me."

"What if we insist?" Isaac, the big Jewish guy, called from the side.

Dad looked at him. Even where we stood at the back of the tent, I could see Dad's eyes were shiny with tears. It took a moment to find his voice. When he did, it was all hoarse. "I know your heart's in the right place, Isaac.

But you, me, all of us, we must be practical. Without Dr. Robbie we cannot continue the project."

"He'll be released," someone called out. "They can't hold him forever."

Dad shook his head. "The problem is . . . Robbie is guilty of the charges. He caused that Jeep to crash and has admitted as much to the authorities."

"But," Samuel argued, "the Johnson camp, they started it. Henderson stole the microchip."

Others agreed more loudly and Dad had to raise his voice to be heard. "I know, I know. But we also know about the government's red tape. If Henderson continues to press charges, it will take weeks, perhaps months to clear Robbie."

There was more than a little unhappiness in the room and Dad had to shout to be heard. "Listen to me. Listen to me!" They finally settled down and he continued. "Should I find more funding, believe me, you'll be the first I contact. But until that time . . ." He took a breath, "Until that time, our work here is finished. Project Truth Seekers is officially closed."

The grumbling grew louder.

"Please!" Dad shouted. "We have run a good race, yes, we have. And I'm sorry things didn't work out. But now I am asking you to pack up your bags and return to your families." His voice was real husky, so before he had a complete melt down he quickly finished, "Thank you, my friends. My thanks to each one of you." Without looking anyone in the eye, he turned and quickly hurried out the side door of the tent.

Jen started after him, but I grabbed her arm. "Where are you going?"

She turned to me, her own eyes filled with tears. "He needs us."

I shook my head.

"What?"

"He needs to be alone," I said. "At least for now. Let him work things out. That's how guys are."

I could tell she didn't like the idea, but for once in her life she seemed to trust me. And that was good, because the meeting wasn't exactly over. Not yet. It's true, people eventually turned and started shuffling out of the tent . . . but then Isaac stopped them.

"Well, I for one am not leaving," he called out.

Several of them turned to listen.

"Dr. Mackenzie is a great man and he's doing a great thing. I'm going to stay with him until he finds funding. I'm going to work for him, even if he can't pay. Who else is with me?"

They hesitated, like they were giving it some thought. But slowly, one by one, they turned and continued towards the exit. Everyone except, Gita. And Hazel who waved her arms and raced toward him shouting, "I'll stay! I'll stay!"

Isaac tried to look pleased at her response, but the guy wasn't going to win any Academy Awards for acting. "Who else?" He called. "Who else will stay with us and support the doctor?"

The rest of the group kept shuffling out the door.

"Come on," he called. "After all he's done for us?"

You could tell they felt bad, their heads down, hands shoved into their pockets. But only one other person remained behind—the guy in the Arab robe and headdress.

"Ibrahim?" Jen whispered to me in surprise.

I shifted my weight and thought, *This should be interesting.*

Isaac must have figured the same thing. "What are you doing?" he demanded.

"What does it appear I am doing?" Ibrahim said. "I am remaining behind to help you."

"We don't need your help."

"That is obvious," Ibrahim answered as he looked about the empty room. "With so many volunteers, I see you have little need for my services."

"We'll be fine," Isaac said.

"Of course." He motioned to Gita and Hazel. "With two women," then he motioned to Jen and me, "and these two children, you have all the help you could possibly need."

"We'll get by without you."

"Without me, perhaps," Ibrahim said. "But without my plan, well, that is another matter."

"Plan?" Hazel asked.

"Plan for what?" Isaac demanded.

"Why, my plan for getting Dr. Robbie out of jail."

CHAPTER TWENTY-SIX

THE BREAK IN

J
A
K
E

"You sure this is the right building?" Isaac asked as the old-fashion elevator slowly rattled up to the third floor.

"Yes, I am certain," Ibrahim said. "My cousin, he is a clerk in this department. When I called, he said this is the place Dr. Robbie is being held for interrogation."

I glanced at Hazel who, luckily, did not have Monkey Boy. Unluckily, she'd just pulled something from her coat called a Time Beam Generator. It looked like a giant flashlight except the lens was full of a hundred smaller lenses, all different colors.

"Well, here we go," she said. She turned on the standby switch and the lenses began to spin.

The good news was Ibrahim had a pretty cool plan, which I'll get to in a sec.

The bad news was Gita didn't think it was so cool. In fact, back at the camp, before we ever got started, she said she didn't think she could help. "God expects us to obey the authorities," she said.

"I get that," Isaac said. "But what if the authorities are wrong?"

"Then we must use the law to show them where they are in error."

Ibrahim stepped in. "But we do not have the time."

"God knows our situation," Gita said. "He knew this would happen long before it ever occurred. If He is in charge, then we must show our trust by going through the proper channels."

Isaac shook his head. "It kills me to say this, but for once I have to agree with Ibrahim. We don't have the time—not even to argue like this. So . . ." he looked over to the rest of us, "who's with me on this and who isn't?"

"I'm in," I said, stepping forward.

"Me too," Hazel chirped. "Oh, this will be so much fun!"

Gita shook her head. "I am sorry, but I cannot be a part of this. Instead, I shall stay behind and attempt to repair the Machine on my own."

Jen was the last to make up her mind. But instead of stepping forward, she just stood there, frowning at the ground.

"Jen?" I asked.

She looked up at me.

"It's for Dad," I said.

She frowned harder, then she looked to Gita and asked, "Do you really think you can fix the Machine without Robbie's help?"

Gita took a deep breath and answered. "There is a slim chance, yes. But it is better to take that chance and do things God's way, than to take a shortcut without Him."

Jen nodded. She paused another second then looked back at me. "I think I'll stay here and help Gita."

I tried to argue. "Jen—"

Isaac cut me off. "It's settled then." He turned to Hazel. "You're sure you can find the right equipment to do this?"

"You betcha," Hazel said, cranking her ever-smile up to a nine and a half.

"Well, then," he said, "let's get going."

They started to leave, but I held back a minute and turned to Jen. "You sure you don't want to come?"

She shook her head.

I gave her one last look. I couldn't put my finger on it, but over the last couple days she seemed to be changing. Who knows, maybe even for the better. Whatever the reason, she stayed back with Gita.

Now Isaac, Ibrahim, Miss Ever-cheer, who'd found Robbie's time beam generator in his pile of junk, and I were riding up the rickety elevator at a police station where they were holding Robbie. The elevator creaked to a stop and the doors rattled open. There in front of us was the reception desk, just like Ibrahim's cousin had said, and beyond that, the door leading to the hallway and jail cells.

The receptionist, a redheaded lady in a police uniform, looked up. "May I help you?" she asked.

"Yes," Isaac said. "We've come to see Dr. Robert P. Ruttledge. We're his legal representatives."

She looked at him questioningly.

Then at Ibrahim and his headdress doubtfully.

Then at me and my age unbelievingly.

Without another word, she reached for a button on her desk.

"She's calling security!" Isaac exclaimed.

"Zap her!" Ibrahim cried.

Hazel didn't need a second invitation. She pointed the time beam generator at the woman and, unable to contain her enthusiasm, giggled, "You're going to really like this!" She flicked the switch and all those spinning lenses in the front lit up like a Christmas tree as the thing began to **HUMMM**.

Uh-oh, I thought. *More* **HUM**-*ming, don't like* **Hum**-*ming,* until suddenly there was a blinding

FLASH

of light. (*Not so fond of those, either.*)

Once it faded, I saw that the receptionist was totally gone. "Where'd she go?" I asked.

Ibrahim turned to Hazel. "What time did you set it for?" he asked.

Hazel grinned. "7:32 AM."

"You transported her back to her home at 7:32 this morning?"

"Oh yes!" Hazel bubbled. "This is such fun!"

Ibrahim, who had walked to the hallway door said, "It

would be more fun if you had allowed her to unlock this before you transported her."

"Oops," she giggled.

"Or if you'd have zapped her *before* she hit the alarm," Isaac said. He motioned to the light above the door that had started flashing red.

"Oh well," she shrugged.

I asked, "Does Robbie have any fancy humming things to break down doors?"

"Don't sweat it," Isaac said, "I have one." He dropped his shoulder and ran at the door full force. It shattered into a million pieces.

"Impressive," Ibrahim said as we stepped through the rubble. We entered a long hallway with ten or so steel doors on each side. They were the type with thick, little glass windows. On the other side of each window you could see the cell where a prisoner was kept.

"You sure about this?" Isaac asked.

Ibrahim nodded. "My cousin is certain he is here."

"We don't have keys to the doors," I said. "And, no offense, but I doubt Isaac's shoulder can handle these."

"No problem," Hazel grinned as she held up the time beam generator. "That's why we've got this little gizmo."

"Let's move!" Isaac ordered, "They'll be here any minute!"

We split up and began checking the cells. Some of them had prisoners, some didn't.

"Here he is!" Hazel shouted. "I found him!" She looked through one of the windows and waved. "Hi Robbie, it's me! How are you? It's really swell to see you!"

We joined her and, sure enough, Robbie was there, shouting back at her. But the glass was too thick to hear.

"Hurry!" Isaac ordered. "Set the coordinates to this morning before he was arrested."

"Already set." Hazel grinned as she pointed the time beam generator through the window at Robbie.

It **HUMMM**–ed and then

FLASH-ed

But when the light faded, nothing had changed.

"What happened?" I asked. "How come he's still there?" I turned to Isaac . . . who *wasn't* there. "Isaac?" I looked back to Hazel. "Where'd he go?"

"The beam," she exclaimed, "the window!"

"What about it?"

"The glass reflected the beam. It bounced off the window, hit Isaac, and, and—"

Ibrahim finished her thought. "—Isaac is back at camp this morning before the arrest?"

Hazel nodded, smiled and looked at the generator in wonder. "Who would have thought?"

"Can you fix it?" I asked.

"Oh sure." She opened a small lid on the side of the generator, and began making adjustments. "I'll have it ready in a jiffy."

We watched as she pulled a screwdriver from her pocket and began screwing screws, switching switches and, er, knobbing knobs.

"Hurry," Ibrahim said as he nervously looked down the hallway. "We must hurry."

"There we go," she finally said as she closed the lid. "Everything's ship-shape and ready for action."

"Quickly," Ibrahim said

"Okee-dokie." Hazel raised the generator back up to the window. It began to **HUMMM** as she pointed it at Robbie. "Smile!" She pressed the button and

FLASH

As the light faded, she looked back through the window. "Uh-oh," she said.

"Uh-oh, what?" Ibrahim asked.

"I may have miscalibrated."

"Did he not go back in time?"

"Yes and no."

I moved to look through the window and saw . . . "A baby?" I shouted. "You replaced Robbie with some baby?"

Hazel glanced back at the time beam generator's controls. "Not exactly *some* baby."

"What did you do?" Ibrahim demanded as he squeezed between us to take a look.

"I forgot to relocate him."

"But why is there a baby?"

"I may have sent him a bit too far back in time."

I turned to her. "So this isn't just any old baby?"

"Oh, no," Hazel smiled. "This is Robbie as a baby." She waved at him through the glass. "Isn't he cute?"

"You turned Dr. Robbie into a baby?" Ibrahim cried.

"Yes." Hazel continued to wave. "Isn't he just the sweetest thing?"

But for two pretty good reasons neither Ibrahim nor I were that impressed.

REASON #1—Dr. Robbie was now Baby Robbie.

REASON #2—Two guards suddenly appeared at the end of the hallway. They were running toward us with raised guns, shouting friendly little things like, "Stop right there! You are under arrest!"

CHAPTER TWENTY-SEVEN

SURPRISING REVELATION

J
E
N
N
I
F
E
R

While Jake and the others were off being heroes, Gita and I focused on the giant electrical circuit Robbie had been work-ing on in the staging area. Of course, part of me wanted to go with Jake and help Robbie escape. I mean it seemed the fastest and most logical way to save Dad's project. But if Gita was right, if that verse about "all things work together for the good" was really true, then maybe her way was the best.

Maybe.

Then there was the deal with Isaac. For some reason he was back with us, which seemed pretty strange because I was sure I saw him leave with the others.

"So why did you come back?" I asked.

"I never left," he said.

"But I saw you."

"You did and you didn't."

I turned to Gita who nodded like she understood. "The time beam generator?" she asked.

"Yeah, probably," he said.

"Probably?" I asked. "Weren't you there?"

"I was and I wasn't."

"But—"

"Long story," he said. "Let's get back to work."

So there we were, the three of us in the hot sun, crawling around the staging area testing the wiring of the giant circuit all by ourselves.

Well, not exactly by ourselves. We still had Maximilian (lucky us). You could tell he missed Hazel. But not as much as he missed the patches of fur we had to shave off him from the bubble gum explosion. The poor thing looked worse than my sixteen-year-old cousin's moth-eaten beard. But that didn't stop him from snooping around and trying to help. No matter how many times I shooed him away, he just kept coming back until, finally . . .

"No, Maximilian!" I shouted as he reached down to touch the bare wires. "Don't—"

ZAP!

He let out a cry and yanked back his hand . . . which was smoking ever so slightly. The good news was the back of his hand and his arm were no longer moth-eaten. The bad news was they were completely bald.

Having learned his lesson, he loped over to join Gita at the control panel where he sat, arms folded, with a definite attitude.

Meanwhile, Gita, Isaac, and I continued checking out each connection . . . one after another, after another.

"How is this one?" Gita called over to me. "Are you receiving a signal?"

I looked down at the voltage meter in my hands and saw the little green lights blinking. "Yes," I said, "the connection is good."

She nodded, entered a few keystrokes and called over to Isaac, "How is that?"

"Yes," he called back. "Good."

And so we continued. It was a long, boring process and would have been faster if Gita and Isaac didn't have to stop every ten minutes to say good-bye to another team member. There were plenty of hugs and more than a few tears as each person swung by to pay his respects. Even though I didn't really know them, it was painful to watch . . . like seeing a family breaking up. And even though Gita and Isaac tried to be all professional, you could tell it was causing them a lot of pain.

But that was nothing compared to the pain I saw just one hour later . . .

Because the midday sun was hot (and none of us wanted to die of sunstroke), we took a break and headed back to our tents.

"We shall resume in ninety minutes," Gita said.

Isaac and I nodded and headed off.

On the way, I thought I'd swing by Dad's just to check up on him. It had been a while since his good-bye speech and I wanted to see how he was holding up. But when I got there and knocked on his door, there was no answer. I knocked again.

"Dad?" I called. "Dad, are you in there?"

Still no answer.

But I heard something. I pushed the door open just a crack. The sound was loud enough to recognize. It was crying. Dad's back was to me so I couldn't see his face, but his head was down on his desk and he was crying. And not just a little. He tried to keep it quiet, but his chest was heaving in huge, gulping sobs.

My heart leaped to my throat.

I didn't know what to do. Part of me wanted to run in and hug him, but another part was scared. I'd never seen him like that. Oh sure, I'd seen him tear up a couple times, but nothing like this. I mean my dad, a grown man, was sobbing like a little boy. It wasn't right. *He's* supposed to be the one in charge. The leader. The rock. *He's* supposed to be the one *we* went to when *we* were sad.

I just stood there, my throat clutched so tight I could barely breathe as my own eyes filled with tears. Slowly, I backed out, making sure he never saw or heard me. Once I was outside, I leaned against the door, all shaky. I wanted to get away, pretend I never saw it. But I couldn't move, not yet. I could still hear him. Faintly. I wanted to cover my ears and make it go away. But I couldn't. I just stood there, hot tears spilling onto my cheeks and running down my face. I tried wiping them away, but the faster I wiped, the faster they came.

CHAPTER TWENTY-EIGHT

REPEAT OF A REPEAT
OF A—

(Well, you get the idea)

J
A
K
E

For those of you keeping score . . .

— We'd broken into an Israeli jail.
— Isaac was zapped back in time to the camp.
— Robbie was zapped back in time to babyhood.
— Two, rather unhappy guards were racing toward us with two rather large guns.

— I was wondering if I was too young to make out
a last will and testament.

I probably left out stuff, but it's hard to remember
everything when you're trying not to wet your pants.

"Uh, Hazel," I said as the bad boys raced towards us,
"you got any ideas?"

"Oh, sure," she said.

"Good."

They kept coming at us.

"Would you mind sharing them?" Ibrahim asked.

"Oh, sure."

They kept coming.

"Now would be a good time," I said.

"Okay." She turned and smiled at our welcoming party
who were about fifty feet away. "Hi guys," she said.

"Throw down the flashlight and put up your hands!"
Bad Boy #1 shouted. Now they were forty feet away.

"Oh, you mean this little thing?" Hazel asked as she
pointed the time beam generator at them.

"Throw it down, now!" Bad Boy #2 ordered.

They were thirty feet away.

She flipped the switch and it **HUMMM**-ed to life.

Twenty feet away.

"Don't you want to see its pretty colors?" she asked.

Ten feet.

"Any time," I said.

She nodded, pulled the trigger and

FLASH

the guards were gone—transported somewhere back in time.

That was the good news. But, of course there was a little

boing . . . oing . . . oing . . . oing . . .

bad.

"What is that sound?" Ibrahim asked.

"Power alarm," Hazel said, glancing at the generator. "The battery is running low."

"But you have enough to make Robbie grow up?" I asked.

"Sure, okay, why not," Hazel said.

Neither Ibrahim or I were thrilled with her answer.

"Hazel?" Ibrahim asked.

"There's only one way to find out," she said. She pointed the time beam generator through the window into Robbie's cell. "After what happened to Isaac, you fellows might want to duck."

Good point. We dropped to our knees and pressed flat against the door as Hazel flipped the switch and the generator began to **HUMMM**. She tapped on the glass to get Baby Robbie's attention. "Say cheese." Then she pulled the trigger and the generator

FLASH-ed

"How is he?" Ibrahim asked as we rose to our feet.

"Oh," Hazel smiled warmly, "what a cutie."

I wasn't crazy about her answer. I was even less crazy when I looked into the window and saw . . .

"A four-year-old?" I cried. "You turned him into a four-year-old!"

Hazel shrugged. "Like I said, we're running out of power. It has to recharge before I can—"

Suddenly the door at the end of the hallway flew open and in ran the same guards as before. Not only were they the same guards, but they were yelling the same thing:

"Stop right there! You're under arrest!"

"Hazel!" Ibrahim shouted.

"You only sent them back a couple minutes?" I cried.

"I told you, we're running out of power."

"Throw down the flashlight and put your hands up!" Bad Boy #1 yelled just like before.

"Send them back," Ibrahim shouted, "send them back!"

They were forty feet away.

"No problem," Hazel said as she pointed the generator at them.

"Throw it down, now!" Bad Boy #2 ordered.

Just like before, she flipped the switch. Only this time the **humm** was a little fainter.

Now they were twenty feet away.

"Look into the pretty light," she said.

Make that ten.

She pulled the trigger and

FLASH

The light was a lot fainter than before but at least they were gone.

Hazel spun the time beam generator back to Robbie's cell and flipped the switch which **humm**-ed even softer.

"Hurry!" Ibrahim shouted.

She pulled the trigger and the

FLASH

was even fainter.

I looked through the window and saw a goofy-looking eleven-year-old geek. "Hazel, he's only—"

The doors at the end of the hall flew open again and again the two guards rushed towards us.

"Stop right there!" they shouted. "You're under arrest!"

"Uh, Hazel?" Ibrahim said.

They were forty feet away when Bad Boy #1 shouted, "Throw down the flashlight and put your hands up!"

"I've seen this show," I shouted. "Can we change channels?"

She nodded, flipped the switch and it **humm**-ed even fainter. And this time when she pulled the trigger it

FLASH-ed

even fainter. It was enough to send the guards back in time, but we all knew not far enough—which explains why Ibrahim stopped Hazel when she tried to point the generator back at Robbie.

"No!" he said, "we have not enough power."

"But—"

"You must use whatever remains to help us escape."

"But—"

"We will return and rescue him another time. This I promise."

Hazel hesitated.

"You have my word. Please, let us go."

Sadly, she raised her hand to the window and waved, "Bye-bye . . ." just as the hallway door flew open and the two guards rushed in shouting, what else, but, "Stop right there! You're under arrest!"

Once again, she spun toward them. Once again she flipped the switch. And once again it humm-ed even softer and it

FLASH-ed

even dimmer.

And, once again, the guards went back in time, but even less far.

"They shall return any second!" Ibrahim shouted. "Let us hurry."

We raced down the hall for the door where the guards would enter. We'd barely made it into the reception area, when we heard the elevator *ding*.

"They're here!" I shouted.

We looked for an exit, but there was none. We were trapped.

"Quickly, take a seat!" Ibrahim shouted. "Look calm!"

Before I could argue, the elevator doors rattled open. With no other choice, I leaped into one of the reception chairs beside Ibrahim and Hazel as she quickly scooped up a magazine and pretended she was reading.

The two guards stormed in. "Where are they?" they demanded.

Hazel looked up from her magazine and casually motioned to the hallway door.

They raced past us and into the hallway. As soon as they entered, Ibrahim jumped from his seat, ran to the door, and slammed it shut, locking it.

"Now what?" I shouted.

Trying his best to sound calm and collected, Ibrahim not-so-quietly suggested: "LET US DEPART FROM THIS PLACE BEFORE WE ARE KILLED!"

It sounded like a pretty good plan.

CHAPTER TWENTY-NINE

TAKE 3

J
E
N
N
I
F
E
R

I was still pretty shook about Dad. Seeing him all broken up like that really hurt. I mean, when you think about it, the poor guy worked most of his life to develop the project, and now, suddenly, the whole thing was pulled out from under him. That's gotta be tough to take and I really did feel bad for him.

But I was also mad. Mad, because I'd never seen him act like that over any of us.

Of course, later, when Jake got back from the jail, he tried to smooth things over . . .

"You never crept up on him like that before," he said. "Maybe he cried the same way over Mom. You know how much he loved her. Maybe he was just hiding it—you know, trying to be strong and tough for us."

I took a breath and blew it out. Maybe. Probably. I didn't know.

Anyway, when Jake and the others arrived and insisted on getting back out to the staging area, I couldn't wait. We didn't tell Dad. Actually, we were afraid to disturb him. But if we could get the Machine up and running and catch Miss Albright before she left the country, all his worries would be over. Of course, Robbie still wasn't with us and we still didn't have the stolen microchip, but maybe this giant circuit thing on the ground would do the trick.

We'd moved the control panel outside the staging area just to be safe. Once everyone was there Ibrahim asked, "Are you positive all circuits have been connected properly?"

"Of course," Isaac answered.

"They have all been tested?"

"I said yes, didn't I?"

"I understand," Ibrahim said, "but sometimes your procedures are not as thorough as—"

"Look," Isaac snapped, "my procedures are as good as any Arab's, all right!"

"Boys, boys," Hazel exclaimed, stepping between them. "Let's think bright and cheery thoughts about each other. What do you say?"

But bright and cheery were definitely not their first thoughts . . . or their last.

Gita cleared her throat and continued her explanation. "We have constructed the circuit as best as we are able, given our limitations. Shall we begin?"

Everyone nodded.

"Please position your goggles."

As we put on our goggles, we looked over to the pedestal with the clay lamp setting on it.

"I just have one question," Hazel asked.

"Yes."

"Why'd you move the control panel out of the staging area?"

Gita explained. "For our first test, I thought it best to simply view what occurs and not endanger ourselves by being a participant."

"But if it's so safe—"

"I did not say it was safe—only that it was the best we can create given our limitations."

We all traded nervous looks.

If Gita saw us, she didn't let on. Instead, she reached down to the control panel, clicked a couple switches and said, "On my mark."

Everyone braced for the worst.

She began counting down, "Five . . . four . . ."

I began praying.

"Three . . . two . . ."

"Commencing firing sequence," Isaac said as he flipped another switch.

". . . one," Gita said. "And mark!"

Just like before, the ray-guns above the lamp began to glow red and the Machine began its strange

oozzza . . . oozzza . . . oozzzza

sound.

"Engaging holographic image!" Gita called as she flipped a final switch.

The air above the staging area crackled like static.

"So far, so good?" Hazel asked.

Gita nodded.

Ever so faintly, we began to hear a crowd. They were cheering, just like before. But, instead of seeing anyone, all we saw was a thick blanket of fog. So thick it was impossible to make out any details except the faint outline of occasional movement.

"What's going on?" Jake asked. "Why can't we see anything?"

Gita entered a few more keystrokes into the computer.

"It's definitely working," Isaac said. "We hear the shouting but—"

"Gita!" Dad came running up from behind us. "What are you doing?"

"We're testing the Machine!" Hazel grinned. "Isn't it fantastic?"

"It's too dangerous!"

Isaac yelled over the growing noise. "We've successfully replaced all elements of the microchip."

"But it's too foggy to see inside," Jake said.

Ibrahim raised his hand. "Please, everyone. Listen to what they are shouting."

We all fell silent. From the fog we could hear them chanting what Dad had recorded the first time . . . only now it was the whole word. "Hosanna!" They yelled. "Hosanna! Hosanna!" There was more, but it was in some weird, foreign language.

"What are they saying?" I asked.

"It is Aramaic," Ibrahim said.

"The translation program," Isaac ordered. "Run it through the translation program."

Gita entered a few keystrokes and suddenly we heard:

"Hosanna! Blessed is He who comes in the name of the Lord! Hosanna!"

Gita cried, "It is Christ's triumphal entry!"

"But we can't see anything!" Isaac yelled. "It will do no good if we can't see it!"

The crowd kept shouting, "Hosanna! The King of Israel! Hosanna!"

"I shall go inside," Ibrahim said. "I shall enter it and verify—"

"No!" Dad said. "It's far too dangerous."

Ibrahim turned to Gita who nodded in agreement. "Dr. Mackenzie is correct. We must run more tests."

"But by then the Albright chick will be long gone," Jake said.

"Your father is correct," Gita repeated. "It is too dangerous."

Jake argued, "But if we can hear them shouting and we know they're in there?"

No one answered.

He turned to me. I saw the look in his eyes. Sometimes twins know exactly what the other is thinking. And I didn't like his thoughts, not one bit. "No, Jake," I said. "No."

He turned back to the fog.

"Jake!"

And then, before anyone could stop him, he bolted towards the staging area.

Dad yelled. "Jake, no!

But it did no good. My impulsive, bull-headed brother had made up his mind. He ducked down his head and ran straight into the fog.

I screamed, "JAAAKEE . . ."

And then he was gone.

"NO!" Dad started after him.

Ibrahim grabbed his arm. "Doctor, you can not go in there."

Dad struggled to get free. "That's my son!"

"Dr. Mackenzie, please!" Gita shouted.

"My son!"

"Dad, please!" I cried.

Then, to everyone's surprise, he leaned back and hit Ibrahim in the face—so hard the man staggered backwards. Dad broke free and ran towards the staging area.

"Dr. Mackenzie!" Everyone was shouting, but it made no difference.

"MY SON!" he cried as he ran into the fog.

"DAD!" I screamed. I started after him but Isaac grabbed me by the waist. "DADDY . . ."

But he did not answer. Just like Jake, he had disappeared.

CHAPTER THIRTY

CLOSE ENCOUNTERS

J
A
K
E

It was just as foggy inside the Machine as it was out. I couldn't see two feet in front of me. There was still plenty of shouting—lots of the "Hosanna!" stuff—along with plenty of clapping and cheering. But I barely saw anyone unless they "OW!" banged into me, or "OUCH!" stumbled over me, or "YEOW!" trampled on my toes.

I tell you, for being projected images, they sure felt real as they kept pushing and shoving their way forward, yelling, "Hosanna! The King of Israel! Hosanna!" And what weird mob scene would be complete without one or two

thwack . . . thwacks . . .

over the head by what looked (and definitely felt) like palm branches?

After a couple minutes of being banged, trampled, and thwacked, I finally heard Dad shouting, "Jake . . . Jake!" He was behind me and pretty close. "Son, can you hear me?"

I spun around, trying to see through the fog. "Dad!"

"Jake?"

"Dad, I'm right here!" I pushed against the crowd, fighting the flood of people.

"Jake?" He was a lot closer.

"I'm right here!"

"Ja—"

"Ow!"

"Is that you, son?"

"Was that your elbow?" I asked, rubbing my gut.

"Sorry."

Finally his face came into view and I threw my arms around him, shouting, "Am I glad to see you!"

"Me, too, son!" He hugged me back (maybe holding me a little longer than necessary). "Me too."

"Where are we?" I yelled as the crowd jostled and swept us along.

"Jerusalem! Palm Sunday!" Dad shouted.

"And everyone's going crazy because they want to see Jesus?"

"Yes and no. They're going crazy because they expect Him to free them from the Romans."

I frowned, trying to remember my Sunday school lessons. "I don't remember Him doing that."

"Because He didn't," Dad yelled. "He's going to free them from something bigger—their sins!"

"By dying on the cross?"

"That's right. In five days He's going to be punished for all we've ever done wrong."

We were interrupted by the voice of some guy shouting. "Out of the way! Step aside!" There was more than the usual shoving and bumping, and for a second I saw a fancy robe brush past me. "Stop this nonsense!" the voice shouted. "Stop it at once!"

I turned toward Dad. "What's going on?"

"Shh," he said, "listen."

"Teacher!" The pushy voice was just ahead of us now. "Teacher!"

The crowd quieted, but only a little.

The voice continued. "Teacher! Rebuke your disciples!"

"Dad, what's happening?

"Listen."

A little farther ahead, I heard another man's voice. It was nothing special—just your common, everyday voice. But there was something about it: strong, but also calm and kind. "I tell you the truth," it answered. Everyone quieted down and it continued. "If these people were silent, the very stones would cry out."

The mob went crazy. They shouted and yelled and clapped . . . and of course, pushed; lots of pushing. Dad reached out and pulled me closer. That's when I saw the tears in his eyes.

"You okay?" I shouted.

He swiped at his face and grinned. But the crowd

surged forward with such force that, before I knew it, we were separated.

"Dad?" I shouted. "Dad!"

I tried pushing back to him, but it did no good. In fact, it caused me to lose my balance. I stumbled and started to fall. I would have caught myself but somebody gave an extra push and I kept going down. The good news was there were plenty of those branches and clothes on the ground to break my fall. The bad news was when I rolled onto my back and looked up, I saw an animal's hoof coming straight towards my head. I froze, not knowing which way to roll. I was blocked by a wall of legs and feet.

"JAKE!"

Everything turned to slow motion: Dad's voice, the approaching hoof, and before I knew it, Dad. He was flying through the fog toward me. He landed hard on my chest and in one continual motion wrapped his arms around me and rolled me to the side . . . just as the hoof came down, barely missing my face.

But not his shoulder.

He cried out in pain as it smashed into him and I heard at least one, maybe two bones give a sickening crunch.

"Dad!"

He did not answer.

"Dad, are you okay?"

"Yeah . . ." he wheezed faintly. But he was lying. I heard it in his voice.

I scrambled to my knees but he just lay there. "What's wrong?" I shouted. "What happened?"

When he didn't answer, I reached down to him. I barely touched him when he screamed in pain. That's when I noticed how wet his shirt was. Warm and wet. I bent my head to take a closer look. The shirt was soaked in blood. Lots of it. And more was coming!

"Dad!"

"I'm . . . okay . . ."

But of course he wasn't. "We have to get you out of here! We have to get you home!"

"Yes . . ." His voice was fainter. I could tell he was losing consciousness.

"How?" I yelled. "Which way do we go?"

"I don't"—he gasped, his voice just a whisper—"know."

CHAPTER THIRTY-ONE

A SURPRISE GUEST

J
E
N
N
I
F
E
R

"Shut it down!" Ibrahim cried out. "Shut it down!"

"It is not responding!" Gita shouted as she flipped dozens of switches all at the same time. "We have a glitch in the system."

"Then cut power!" Isaac yelled.

"The shock will be too great," Gita cried. "It will harm their limbic systems."

"Not as much as dying!"

"I assure you, no one will be dy—"

She was interrupted by Jake's voice shouting from inside the fog. "Gita!" You could barely make him out over the noise of the crowd, but it was definitely him. "Gita! Can anybody hear me?"

I spun to Gita. "That's my brother!" I turned back to the staging area and yelled, "Jake? Jake, we're right here!"

He continued shouting, "I don't know if you can hear me, but Dad—he's hurt real . . ." His voice faded into the shouts of the crowd.

"Jake, we hear you!" I yelled. "What's wrong? What happened to Dad? Jake!"

There was no answer—just the sound of the crowd.

"He can't hear us," Isaac said. "There's too much noise."

I turned back to Gita, who madly worked the controls trying to dial Jake's voice in more clearly.

". . . losing lots of blood . . . gotta get him out . . ."

I turned to the others. "What happened? What's going on?"

"Some sort of accident," Hazel shouted.

"Shut it down!" Ibrahim ordered.

"If I do, we could lose them both!" Gita exclaimed.

"Somebody do something!" I yelled.

Jake's voice continued, "Not sure where to go . . . too many . . ."

"All right, fine!" Ibrahim said. He broke from us and headed for the staging area.

"What are you doing?" Isaac yelled.

"I shall go myself."

"And get lost like them?"

"No!" Gita continued working the controls. "It is too dangerous."

But Ibrahim didn't stop. "We have no other choice."

"I said, no!" For the first time I can remember, Gita sounded angry.

But he kept going.

"As your superior, I forbid it!" Gita shouted. "Is that clear?"

Ibrahim slowed just a few feet from the edge of the fog. It was obvious he didn't want to go against her orders, but it was also obvious he had to help.

"Gita!" Jake kept yelling. "Can anybody hear me?"

To make matters worse, the chimpanzee started acting up—hooting, hollering, and making a real fuss.

"Maximilian, no!" Hazel shouted.

But something behind us had gotten his attention and he wouldn't let up.

"Please tell your monkey to stop!" Isaac yelled.

"He's not a monkey, he's a chimpanzee!" Turning back to him, Hazel shouted, "Maximilian, no!"

Instead of stopping, Maximilian raced from the group and ran toward the supply trucks parked behind us. But he wasn't running toward the trucks, he was running toward the person snooping around them. Some guy. I squinted against the sun. It was Jesse! The boy from the hilltop. He'd set something down on one of the fuel barrels and was turning to run off. But Maximilian had spotted him and was hot on his tail.

Hazel started after him. "Maximilian!"

But Maximilian was in no mood to stop. He gained ground on Jesse and probably would have caught him if Jesse hadn't disappeared behind one of the trucks. A moment later he roared out on a motorbike. He zoomed past the chimp, barely missing him, and took off, leaving him in a cloud of dust. Of course, Maximilian raced after him, but it was a losing battle as Jesse sped away, out into the desert.

"Maximilian!" Hazel shouted. "Maximilian!"

At last the animal came to a stop. He slapped the ground several times in frustration then turned and loped back to us. But not before Hazel approached the fuel barrel to see what the boy had left behind.

"What is it?" Isaac called.

"It's the circuit!" She picked it up and waved it at us. "It's the microchip they stole."

"Bring it here!" Isaac yelled. "Let's see if we can use it!"

Hazel ran back and handed the microchip to Gita, who gave it a quick inspection. When she was satisfied she passed it to Isaac, who raced to the front of the control panel, opened a compartment door, and inserted it.

Meanwhile, Jake continued shouting. "Can anybody hear me? Gita . . . Jen . . ."

Isaac closed the door and called, "All set!"

Gita nodded. She entered a bunch of keystrokes and once again the Machine began to

oozzza . . . oozzza . . . oozzzza

though the sound was a lot softer than usual.

The air began to *sizzle* and *crackle* over the staging area as we stared into the fog, waiting and watching. But nothing happened.

"It is not working," Ibrahim cried.

Isaac read the meters on the control panel. "We don't have enough power."

"Disengage the old circuit," Gita ordered.

Isaac nodded and flipped several switches. "Disengaging."

Almost immediately the

oozzza . . . oozzza . . . oozzzza

grew to its regular volume.

Then, with one last *sizzle*, and a couple more *crackles*, the fog vanished.

Now we could see the crowd. It was huge. The people were shouting and waving palm branches along a dirt road that lead to some ancient city with a wall. A wall that looked a lot like the one Gita had pointed out when we'd driven past Jerusalem to the airport.

But the crowd and wall were not my worry. "Where are they?" I shouted. "Where's Dad, where's Jake?"

"Standby." Gita adjusted more controls until, suddenly

oozzzzzzzzzzzzzzz

all the sounds and all of the images faded. The staging area was completely empty . . . except for Jake and Dad standing near the middle.

I bolted towards them. But I wasn't as fast as the others who quickly surrounded them. Still, I caught glimpses of Dad's blood-soaked shirt and I went cold.

"Give me a hand," Isaac ordered Ibrahim. "Let's get this shirt off him. He's losing too much blood!"

They ripped away Dad's shirt. The hole in his shoulder was deep and ugly. I felt my head growing light. But I forced myself to watch as Ibrahim yanked off his precious headdress, wadded it into a ball, and shoved it into Dad's open, bleeding wound.

"What happened?" Gita asked.

"He got stomped on by a horse," Jake said.

"A donkey," Dad wheezed. Even though he was barely conscious and in a lot of pain, you could hear the excitement in his voice.

"A donkey?" Hazel asked.

"It was Palm Sunday," Jake said.

Hazel's jaw slacked. "Do you think . . . could it have been—"

"The donkey Jesus rode?" Ibrahim asked.

Dad tried to answer but it sent him into a fit of coughing.

Isaac ordered, "Gita, grab his legs. Let's get him out of the sun and into a tent."

"Let me help," Jake said. But as soon as they pulled Dad away, he crumpled to the ground.

"Jake!" I dropped down to join him.

"I'm okay," he mumbled. "Just a little woozy."

"It's shock," Isaac said. "Somebody give him a hand."

Hazel joined me and the two of us helped him to his feet.

"I'm cool," he said, "everything's good."

But he wasn't good. I could tell by the way he had to lean on us for support.

It took a couple minutes to carry them to the nearest tent. Hazel found some gauze and disinfectant. Then she, Isaac, and Ibrahim began working on Dad, cleaning the wound and trying to stop the bleeding. I wanted to watch, but this time I knew I'd pass out so I turned away.

Jake was stretched out on a nearby cot so I sat next to him. He looked real tired and his eyes were all red and puffy.

"What happened?" I asked.

"Let him rest," Isaac called. "There'll be plenty of time to talk later."

I nodded and started to rise when Jake grabbed my arm. He tried to sit up but couldn't. His voice was thick and raspy. "He saved me. I could have been killed, but he . . ." Jake swallowed and continued, "Dad risked his life to save mine."

I stared down at my brother, watching tears fill his eyes. Jake never cried, but when he did it usually wiped me out too.

"For me," he croaked. "He was going to die for me."

That did it. My own eyes brimmed with tears.

"Jennifer." The sternness in Isaac's voice said he meant business. "Let him rest."

I looked down at Jake. Swallowing back the knot in my throat, I tried to smile. "Get some rest," I whispered. "You've been through a lot."

He nodded and closed his eyes.

I looked over to Dad. Isaac, Ibrahim, and Hazel were still hovered over him and working away. But not Gita. She was nowhere to be seen. I rose and moved across the tent, still thinking of Jake's words. It was true, Dad loved

us. I knew that. Maybe he was too busy to show it, maybe
he didn't always know how to show it. But he loved us. So
much he was willing to die for us.

Outside, I spotted Gita sitting on a nearby bench. Her
head was bowed and her hands folded. When she heard
me, she looked up and smiled. Then she scooted over so I
could sit beside her.

"Is he . . ." my voice clogged. "Will he be okay?"

She nodded. "Isaac is a medical doctor. He knows what
to do."

A gigantic weight rolled off my chest. *Thank you, God.*
Thank you. We sat in silence for a while. When I stole a
glance to Gita, she was looking over to the Machine and
staging area.

"What?" I asked.

She turned to me and smiled. "It works. After all of
these years, your father's efforts have finally paid off."

"But with no one to fund it, what good will it do?"

She nodded slowly and sadly.

"Miss Albright—she's long gone by now?" I asked.

Gita glanced at her watch. "She should be boarding her
plane any time now."

I sighed. "And we can't call her because we managed to
destroy her cell phone."

Gita nodded.

"So there's no way to reach her."

"That is correct."

But even as we sat there, a thought was coming to my
mind. "Unless . . ."

She looked at me.

"What about the dimensional folder?" I asked. "Wouldn't that get us to the airport in time?"

"Within seconds." Then Gita shook her head. "But it takes two—one to operate and one to be transported. Everybody is busy with your father."

"Not you and me."

"You do not know how to operate it."

"You do."

She turned to me. "You would be willing to be transported?" Before I could answer, she shook her head. "No, it is too risky. For you, there is too much danger."

"Why do you say that?"

"The winged creature appears to you whenever the dimensional folder is engaged."

"So . . ."

"So for you to participate, to be involved in the actual operation—" Again she shook her head.

I took a breath. She was right, of course. But she'd also been right about something else. I hesitated, then answered, "We beat it before, that shadow thing—a couple times."

"This is true, but you have never crossed dimensions. You have never been that close to its operation."

I swallowed. "What did you tell me? We have the authority, isn't that what you said? We have the authority, we just need to put our faith in God?"

"Yes, but—"

"Why is now any different from then?"

She turned and looked at me long and hard. "Can you, in all honesty, tell me that you have that type of faith?"

I took another breath, deeper this time. Part of me wanted to say no, to run and hide. But there was another part, the part that had seen so many things since I'd been there: Gita's faith, the real Jerusalem, the real Palm Sunday . . . and the real love and faith of everyone around me . . . including my father's.

Finally, I answered. "Dad put his whole life into this project. Isn't this the least I can do?" I gave another swallow. "For him?"

"You may have to face that creature . . . all by yourself."

I looked down and stared hard at the ground. "No . . . not by myself." Then looking back up to her, I added, "I have God."

Gita stared at me another long moment. Then, ever so slowly, so small you could barely see it, she started to nod.

I tried to smile, but didn't quite pull it off. I gave another swallow, but my mouth was as dry as the sand around us.

CHAPTER THIRTY-TWO

ENCOUNTER!

J
E
N
N
I
F
E
R

Gita stood at the glowing table inside the lab prepping the dimensional folder. Of course I had a gazillion questions to ask her, but the biggest one was, "Are you sure all the bugs are worked out?"

"Yes," she said. "After the incident involving Isaac and Ibrahim, we have checked it thoroughly."

That gave me some comfort, because if there was one

thing Gita couldn't do, it was lie. Of course, there was still my worry over the shadow thing the dimensional folder might stir up. But as nervous as I was, I couldn't help thinking about Jesse and the microchip. Did he have it all along? Did he go back to the wrecked Jeep and find it? Then there was the even bigger question:

Why?

Why did he bring it back? Was it because of . . . I pushed the thought out of my mind, but it kept returning. Was it because of me? Okay, maybe that was just a dream, but it was a good one . . . and it helped take my mind off what was about to happen.

Gita kept working the computer keyboard and giving me last-minute instructions. "According to my information, Miss Albright is flying El Al Airlines from Tel Aviv to New York City."

I nodded.

"I am able to transport you to the airport, even to the appropriate gate. However, you must be the one to personally approach her and convince her to return."

"I understand."

Without looking up from her work, Gita continued. "Please check your communication device." I pressed the little hearing aide against my ear as she kept talking. "Check one, two, three . . . can you hear me?"

I nodded.

"Good. And may I hear you, please?"

I dropped my head down to the little microphone she'd pinned to my shirt. "Test one, two."

"Excellent. I hear you loud and clear."

I nodded, my heart pounding so loud I figured she

probably heard that too. At last, she looked up from the computer terminal and smiled. "It is time. Are you certain you are ready?"

If I thought about what we were doing, I'd freak out. But if I thought about Dad and Jesse and the project . . . and the authority Gita said I had over that creepy creature, I was okay. I took a deep breath and nodded.

"Excellent. Step onto the platform, please."

I looked down at the triangle with the lights flashing around it. I tried raising my foot to step onto it, but my leg wouldn't cooperate. It was like my brain was saying yes, but my body had other ideas. Maybe it knew something I didn't.

"Jennifer?"

I focused on my foot, concentrating, until I was finally able to lift one leg onto the platform. Then my other. Gita entered a few more keystrokes and everything started to hum as the lights around it began flashing faster.

"Stand by."

My heart pounded like a jackhammer on too many cups of coffee. *Dear Jesus,* I silently prayed. *Help me do this. Help me have the courage to—no, help me have the* faith *to do this.*

Gita entered a few more keystrokes, looked up to me and smiled. "Godspeed, Jennifer Mackenzie." Then she hit one, final key. The cross-dimensional folder

CRACKLE-ed

loudly, gave a blinding FLASH of light and suddenly I was flying.

At least that's what it felt like. And looked like. It reminded me of those time-lapse photos of the night sky with all the streaks of stars and planets . . . only these streaks weren't standing still—they were zooming past me!

"Gita!"

"Do not worry," she answered calmly through my earpiece. "You are only folding dimensions."

"I'm supposed to be at the airport!" I yelled, "not, not—"

"Outer space?" she offered.

"OUTER SPACE?"

"Perhaps it's best you close your eyes through this process."

"CLOSE MY EYES?"

"Otherwise I am afraid you will become more frightened."

"MORE FRIGHTENED?" I know I sounded like a parrot, repeating everything I heard, but it was the best I could do under the circumstances.

Figuring she knew better, I closed my eyes. A moment later I heard something—quiet at first, but growing louder by the second. Louder and more beautiful. The truth is, I'd never heard anything like it.

"Gita," I asked, "is that . . . singing?"

"Yes."

It was impossible to describe—so gorgeous that I wanted to laugh and cry all at the same time.

"What is it?" I asked. "Who is it?"

"We have been unable to verify the source. However, since you are folding into higher dimensions, there is a slight chance you may be entering—"

There was a blaze of whiteness. And then another. And another. Not a flash of light, but just . . . white. Along with it came something I could feel. It brushed against my face, but it didn't hurt. Instead, it felt soft and fluffy. It gently wrapped around me, like a tender hug. I knew Gita was right, I should probably keep my eyes shut, but I had to see what was going on. Ever so slightly, I squinted them open. Then I gasped.

"Gita . . . are these feathers?"

She didn't answer.

My mind raced—higher dimensions, beautiful singing, white feathers. "Gita, are these . . . am I with angels?"

She continued to ignore me. "You shall be dropping back into our dimension shortly. But you must pass through one more. And for this one, please, I am very serious, you must keep your eyes closed."

"Why? Where am I going?"

"We are not certain, but you will be safe. Trust me."

"But—"

"Jennifer, please."

"All right," I said, "all right." I closed my eyes. The white and sensation of feathers faded. Soon I was in total darkness. No feathers. No singing. Nothing but blackness . . . and then something else. Low and gravely. Like the sound of animals.

"Gita? Is that growling?"

"You will pass through this quickly, I promise."

"Pass through *what*?"

The growling grew louder. I noticed a red light flickering against my eyelids, like fire. But there was no heat. I was desperate to look, but Gita knew me too well. I was just about to open my eyes when she repeated, "No, Jennifer! Do not!"

The growling became louder . . . along with it, those clicking and clacking sounds, like I'd heard from the winged shadow, only this time there were lots more of them. My whole body tensed. I was terrified. I had to look. Just one peek. Just one—

And then I heard a woman's voice. She was talking through a speaker in a big room with other voices in the background. Normal light replaced the red flickering and I felt the wonderful coolness of air-conditioning wash over my body. The voice grew clearer.

"Final call for Flight 108 to Kennedy International Airport. All passengers should now be on board."

I opened my eyes and, sure enough, I was back in the middle of Tel Aviv's Ben Gurion International Airport. I glanced around the terminal and saw the door to the nearest boarding ramp. It was labeled GATE 7.

"I'm here!" I shouted. Then seeing everyone turn and stare at me, I lowered my voice and whispered into my shirt. "Gita, I'm here."

"Excellent," she replied.

"Gate 7?" I asked. "Is she leaving from Gate 7?"

"According to my information."

"Perfect." I raced for the door. But as I approached, I saw a sign above it reading: LONDON: HEATHROW. Confused, I turned to the gate attendant and asked, "Excuse me. That says London. Shouldn't it be New York?"

She looked up from her work and frowned.

I motioned to the gate. "Shouldn't that say New York?"

"There's been a gate change." She typed something into her computer and read it. "The flight to New York has been moved to Gate 49."

"Gate 49!" I turned and looked down the terminal. It stretched on forever.

"I should hurry if I were you," the woman said as she returned to her work. "They'll be closing the door shortly."

Without a word, I spun around and started running down the terminal for all I was worth. I passed Gate 8. Then Gate 9. But 49 was so far away. At this rate I'd never make it.

If that wasn't bad enough, I noticed another little problem. At first I thought the shadow against the windows was from a passing cloud. But when I turned for a better look, I saw there were no clouds . . . and it wasn't exactly a shadow.

It was the giant winged creature outside. And it was tracking with me.

CHAPTER THIRTY-THREE

FAITH IN ACTION

J
E
N
N
I
F
E
R

"Gita!" I cried. "It's here! The thing is here!"

"It must have followed you through dimensions."

"What do I do?"

"Do not panic. Remember you have the authority."

"Yes, but—"

"You must use your faith, Jennifer. Put your trust in Jesus."

As soon as Gita said the name *Jesus*, the thing turned its head and looked directly at me. I heard what sounded like a screech as it changed course and shot straight through the window. But the glass didn't break. It passed through it as easily as light . . . pitch-black light.

Now it headed directly for me.

I desperately searched the terminal, looking for a place to run, to hide. Just ahead was a restroom. I cut to the left and made a beeline for it. All the time Gita was calling through my earpiece, "Jennifer, Jennifer, can you hear me?"

But I had no time to answer.

I threw open the door, startling four or five women at the sinks and mirror. I spotted an empty stall at the far end and raced for it. Once inside I locked the door and leaned against the wall, trying to catch my breath. I held it a moment and listened. I heard the sound of claws scraping across tile. With it came that awful clicking and clacking. It moved to the stalls, peering into first one and then another, coming closer and closer.

"Jennifer . . ." Gita kept calling through my earpiece, "Jennifer, are you all right?"

The clicking and clacking stopped.

"Jennifer . . ."

It must have heard her.

"Jennifer . . ."

I pulled out the earpiece and covered it with my hands, trying to muffle her voice. But it did no good.

"What is happening?"

I looked around and saw the toilet. There was no other choice. I dropped it into the bowl. Tiny bubbles rose from it as it drifted to the bottom. Now it was silent.

Now I was alone.

The clicking and clacking resumed. It grew louder as it checked stall after stall.

I pressed against the wall, silently praying. *Dear Jesus, what do I do?*

The thing was two, maybe three stalls away.

I wrapped my arms around myself and slid silently to the floor. Then I heard it in the very next stall.

What do I do?

There was silence. I knew I shouldn't, but I had to look. I tilted up my head and there it was, leering down at me.

"Jesus . . ." I gasped.

It drew back, looking startled.

I was surprised as it was. I said the name again. "Jesus."

It shook its head back and forth, like someone had punched it. And that was all I needed to see. I said the name louder. "Jesus!"

It glared down at me, looking like it wanted to strike. But it didn't. It couldn't.

What had Gita said? *You are the one with the power . . . if you put your faith in Jesus.*

I raised my chin and spoke louder. "In the name of—"

My voice caught and I tried again. "In the name of Jesus Christ, I demand that you go!"

The shadow rippled. It pulled its head farther away like it was the one who was afraid. *Really? Afraid? Of me?* But of course it wasn't me. It was who was with me. I started to inch up and it pulled farther away. Finally I had the courage to rise to my feet. It ducked back behind the door, out of sight. But it was still there. I could feel it.

I reached for the latch. My hand was trembling as I unlocked it. *You are the one with the power.*

Then, ever so cautiously, I pushed it open. The thing hissed like an angry cat, pulling back even further. I took a breath and spoke again, louder. "In the name of Jesus Christ . . . I order you to go!"

By now all the ladies around the sinks were staring. They figured I'd lost my mind. But it didn't matter. I didn't care what they thought, what anybody thought. Jesus was with me. I had His authority. I had the authority of the Son of God and nothing would stop me.

"Now!" I shouted.

The thing rippled faster. It spread out its wings trying to look scarier.

"Now!" I yelled. "In the name of Jesus Christ, I command you to go!"

A cry began somewhere deep inside it. It rose to a desperate scream. As it rose, the darkness began breaking apart. The scream grew into an earsplitting shriek.

"NOW! IN JESUS' NAME, GO!"

Suddenly the thing exploded. Pieces of shadow flew in all directions. And as they flew, they quickly faded away . . . along with the scream. Within seconds, there was nothing left—no sound, no shadows, nothing—except some very confused old ladies.

There was no time to waste. I ran past them, threw open the door and raced back into the terminal. I still had to get to Miss Albright. But I was only at Gate 11. With all the time wasted, there was no way I could reach Gate 49. Still, I ran, passing Gate 12, then 13.

I'd lost Gita's earpiece but I still had her microphone so I lowered my head to my shirt and shouted, "Gita, I don't know if you can hear me, but they changed gates! The plane is at Gate 49 and I'm at 13. I can't make it! They're going to depart and I can't get there in time! They're going to—"

Suddenly a thought surfaced. It was a terrifying idea, but the only one that made sense. "Gita, can you cross-dimensionalize me into the plane before it leaves?" I couldn't believe I was saying it, but it was our only hope. "Can you get me inside that plane before it takes off so I can—

I heard a *CRACKLE*, saw a blinding FLASH, and I was in darkness.

Yes! She must have thought the same thing! I was both excited and scared. I closed my eyes and this time kept them shut—through the brightness, the feathers, the darkness, the flickering red light, until suddenly—

There I was, standing in the aisle of a crowded plane. I opened my eyes and blinked, trying to get my bearings. With all the big, fancy seats, I figured I was in first class. I quickly scanned them, looking for Miss Albright.

"Excuse me," It was a flight attendant behind me. "Excuse me, young lady!"

I ignored her, continuing to look.

"You must take your seat before we close the cabin door."

Then I spotted her, three rows back. "Miss Albright!"

The woman looked up, startled, from her magazine as I approached.

"I'm Jennifer Mackenzie, Dr. Mackenzie's daughter."

She raised her chin in that usual snootiness and said, "I know precisely who you are." As if remembering our last encounter, she self-consciously checked her hair.

"You have to come with me," I said. "The Machine's working. You have to—"

"Miss," the flight attendant ordered, "you must take your seat."

"It's working!" I repeated. "Everything's working!"

The attendant took my arm and spoke to Miss Albright. "Excuse, me, ma'am, is she with you?"

Miss Albright shook her head. "She most certainly is not."

The attendant began to pull. "Then you must come with me."

"But—"

"If you refuse to take your seat, you will be escorted from the plane."

I dug in my heels. "Miss Albright, you have to believe me."

The old woman looked at me another moment, then shook her head and returned to her magazine.

"Young lady, I'm going to have to call security."

I stood helplessly, unsure what to do . . . until the old lady gave another self-conscious check of her hair. And then I had it! In one quick move, I lunged forward, grabbed Miss Albright's wig, and ripped it off.

She let out a scream and tried to cover herself.

The flight attendant was so startled I slipped from her grasp and raced for the door. There was all sorts of yelling and shouting behind me, but I had the element of surprise.

I raced out of the plane, down the boarding ramp, and into the terminal.

I kept going another fifty feet before I slowed to a stop and waited, holding the wig in my hand. Sure enough, just as I hoped, Miss Albright came out, still covering her head. The flight attendant was at her side.

"We must depart now," the attendant was explaining. "We must close the door and—"

"Not without my hair!" Miss Albright shouted.

"But—"

Then Miss Albright spotted me. "You!" She yelled. "Stay right there!" She started for me. "Do not move! Do you hear me?"

"Ma'am?" the attendant called after her. "Ma'am!"

But Miss Albright would not be stopped. She kept heading toward me, yelling and shouting. And I just stood there, holding her wig like bait . . . as, behind her, the flight attendant finally sighed, reached for the gate door, and closed it.

I had her! There would be lots of explaining to do, and even more apologizing, but I had Miss Albright!

CHAPTER THIRTY-FOUR

AT LONG LAST . . .

J
A
K
E

Dad waved at Miss Albright. "Are you sure you don't want to join us inside the staging area?"

"I am perfectly content to stand out here and watch," she said.

"All right, I understand."

And he did understand. After all we'd put the old girl through, we were just happy she'd come back. Not that *she* was particularly happy. But after promising to keep the monkey locked up and to put her on the first plane home tomorrow, she agreed to give us one more try.

And we were ready to rock!

"Is everybody set?" Gita asked from the control panel.

We nodded.

"Then please, lower your goggles."

We all obeyed. Earlier, we'd moved the control panel back inside the staging area. That way if there were any more little surprises . . . like fog covered cities or rampaging dinos, Gita and Isaac could bail us out. Of course, it would have been cooler to have Robbie with us, but he was still back at the jail messing with everybody's head as a teenager. We'd figure a way to spring him out, but right now we had bigger fish to fry.

"On my mark," Gita said.

Of course we tried to convince Dad to stay in bed. It had only been a day since the accident. But there was no way he was going to miss the show. So we put his arm in a sling and Ibrahim dug out an old wheelchair so he could roll him into the staging area with the rest of us for the fun and games.

Gita began counting down. "Five . . . four . . ."

I took a deep breath and threw a look over to Jen. She was doing the same.

"Three . . . Commence firing sequence."

Isaac nodded and hit a bunch of switches.

"Two . . . one. Mark!"

The ray-guns above the clay lamp began their creepy, red glow, along with their creepier

oozzza . . . oozzza . . . oozzzza

"Engaging holographic image," Isaac called as he switched a final switch.

The air crackled around us and, just like that, we were standing in the middle of the same crowd Dad and I had been in the day before. Only this time we could actually see something! There were hundreds of men, women, and little kids. Everyone was smooshed together along a dirt road and shouting, "Hosanna! Hosanna!" Some had those crazy palm branches we'd seen earlier and were waving them like banners.

"Everybody okay?" Ibrahim shouted above the noise.

We were getting jostled around pretty good, but no one was complaining.

"You sure they can't see us?" Jen yelled.

"Yes," Gita shouted from the control panel, which was also surrounded by the crowd. "Everything we see is merely a holographic projection."

"But be careful," Dad warned from his chair. "Remember, it's so real our bodies act as if it *is* real."

I nodded, remembering all too well, as the crowd got more and more worked up, everyone shouting, "Hosanna! The king of Israel!" There was movement up ahead and I craned my neck for a better look. People were parting, letting someone pass through. "Hosanna! Hosanna!"

Then I got a peek. The man who was the center of attention wasn't walking. He was sitting, riding on a donkey. The crowd continued to part until I saw more of His robe, then His dark hair, and finally His beard, before He was blocked from my view again.

By now everyone was going wild. Some had ripped off their coats or whatever and were throwing them on the ground in front of the donkey. "Hosanna!" they yelled. "Blessed is He who comes in the name of the Lord!"

More people stepped back until I finally got a long, clear look at Him. *That's it?* I thought. *You're kidding me.*

He's just a man. No halo. No glowing white clothes. No choir of singing angels. Just a regular guy smiling and waving. But that didn't stop the coats from flying and the palm branches from waving. "Hosanna! Hosanna! Hosanna!"

Then, just like yesterday, I heard another voice behind me. "Move! Get out of the way!" I turned to see three guys decked out in fancy robes. "Step aside!" They pushed their way past me and started yelling at the man on the donkey, yelling at Jesus. "Stop this at once! Teacher, stop this!"

They were fifteen feet away and I could clearly see Jesus' face. Like I said, there was really nothing special about Him . . . except for those eyes. They were sharp and clear, and majorly kind. You could tell He really enjoyed being with the people . . . but you could also see there was something else. A sadness—like He knew what they were going to do to Him in just a few days.

The tallest of the fancy robes stepped in front of the donkey, forcing it to stop. "Teacher," he shouted, "rebuke your disciples!"

Jesus looked at him, and you could see that sadness again. Finally He spoke. It was the same voice I'd heard yesterday. Again, nothing fancy, but clear and kind and totally calm.

"I tell you the truth." He motioned to the people who were settling down and growing quiet. "If these were silent, the very stones would cry out." With that He nudged the donkey forward. The crowd went crazy, shouting and clapping as the dude in the fancy robes had to step out of the way or get run over.

That's when it dawned on me; Jesus was riding toward me. He'd be coming so close, I could actually reach out and touch Him. I spun around to Dad, making sure he was taking it all in. But I could barely see him. He was in the wheelchair, his view completely blocked by the crowd.

I turned back to Jesus. He was ten feet away. Seriously, in half a minute I'd be face-to-face with Jesus Christ!

"Hosanna!" the crowd kept shouting. "Hosanna! Hosanna!"

But what about Dad? I turned and saw him fighting to get up from the chair, but he couldn't.

"Hosanna! Hosanna!"

That's when I knew. Even though I might totally miss Jesus passing, I knew what I had to do. I turned and pushed my way through the crowd toward Dad. Once I got there, I reached down to help him stand.

"Jake," he shouted, "what are you doing? You're going to miss Him!"

"Come on," I shouted as I helped him to his feet. "Come on!"

Together we began pushing our way back through the crowd. I could hear him gasping in pain, but I knew he didn't want to stop. This was more important than his pain, this was something he'd worked his whole life for.

Finally we reached the edge of the path. Jesus was only six feet away, smiling and waving to the crowd. Make that four feet. I glanced to Dad. Tears streamed down his face. I'd never seen him so happy. "Jesus," he whispered. "Jesus . . . Jesus . . ." As the crowd kept shouting, "Hosanna . . . Hosanna!"

Of course I hoped He'd see us—that we'd catch Jesus' eye and He'd give us a nod or something. But, like Gita said, He was just a holographic projection; there was no way He could see us. But then, the strangest thing happened.

He was just three feet away, passing us. He was waving to the crowd when the sleeve of His robe accidentally brushed against Dad's bad shoulder. It was only for a second and of course He didn't notice. I barely did.

But Dad did. Big time. "He touched me!" he gasped.

I nodded, watching as Jesus passed and continued up the path toward the city.

"Jake, He touched me!"

"Yeah," I grinned. "Pretty cool."

"No, you don't understand."

I turned to him.

"My shoulder . . ." Dad pulled his arm out of the sling and moved it.

No way! I thought. The pain alone should have wiped him out. Instead, he was grinning ear to ear. "Jake . . . my shoulder!" He rolled it a little. Then an idea came to him. He quickly unbuttoned his shirt and reached for the bandage.

"Dad!" I shouted, "Don't—"

But I was too late. He'd ripped it off.

And to our amazement, there was no blood. There was no wound. There wasn't even a scar. It was like he'd never been hurt.

CHAPTER THIRTY-FIVE

WRAPPING UP

J
E
N
N
I
F
E
R

"Have a great flight!" Dad yelled over the pounding of the helicopter blades.

"Of course I will!" Miss Albright shouted with her usual snootiness. "After all, I am flying first class."

Jake and I traded looks. Some things never change.

She took Dad's arm as he helped her up into the passenger seat. "My lawyers will have the papers drawn up and a check to you within the week. I trust you can wait that long."

Dad grinned. "I am so appreciative, Miss Albright. With that money we can finally finish the project and reach the entire world with God's truth."

Raising her chin she said, "With that amount of money, I expect to make much, much more of it."

Dad gave a sad sort of smile. Making money was the last thing on his mind, but apparently the first on Miss Albright's. At least for now. He shut her door and slapped it with his hand, signaling Hazel that it was safe to take off. Wearing her perma-grin, Hazel leaned past Miss Albright, gave a thumbs-up, and pushed the throttle forward. Miss Albright cut a glance to her. Even with her nose in the air, she didn't look all that relaxed.

But at least Maximilian was out of her hair (or wig). Jake was holding him on a leash as he kept jumping up and down (Maximilian, not Jake) and doing his usual

"Oo-ooo . . . Aah–aah . . . Eee-eee-ing!"

"Hey, Monkey Boy!" Jake tugged on the leash. "Chill!"

But true love knows no bounds. As the helicopter rose into the air and Miss Albright glanced at us one final time, Maximilian blew a bubble, raised his eyebrows up and down, and gave her a wink. The old lady looked away, obviously unnerved.

Meanwhile Dad had stepped back to join Jake and me. "Well, that's that!" he shouted.

"Good riddance!" Jake agreed.

Dad grinned and pulled him into a hug. Then he reached out his other arm for me. I hesitated—I don't know why, maybe it was from all the past years—but it was only a second, before I stepped in and let him hold me. It felt terrific, like I was a little kid, again, snuggling into his arms. He must have felt it, too, because he pulled me even closer.

Did we still have issues? You bet. Was I thrilled to be stuck out in this desert? Not even. But what was it Gita said? "All things work together for the good to those who love the Lord." She was right. Not all things were good, but all things worked together for the good. And there, in my dad's arms, with my brother on his other side, I didn't doubt it, not for a second.

As we watched the helicopter pull away, I noticed a glint of reflection on top of the mountain above the camp. I shaded my eyes, squinting against the rising sun. It looked like a motorcycle. And though I couldn't be sure, I had a pretty good idea who the rider was. At least who I hoped he was. Hmm, maybe hanging around this place wouldn't be so bad after all. We'd see.

"What on earth?"

I glanced over to Dad who was looking down at his feet. Two desert scorpions were scurrying past us toward the camp. Jake lifted up his boot to crunch them, but Dad grabbed his arm. "No, wait."

Jake looked up to him. "What?"

Dad motioned further ahead where two hyraxes (furry-looking animals, like fat rabbits but without ears) were also scampering toward the camp. "And over there." He pointed to a couple goats approaching.

"And up there." Gita pointed at the sky where two hawks were swooping past, followed by a couple owls, and then two pigeons—all of them heading in the same direction.

"What's going on?" I asked.

"Oh, brother." Isaac motioned down the hill toward the Machine.

We turned and were totally surprised to see a giant boat the size of a cruise ship sitting in the middle of the staging area. Around it, other animals were approaching—two gazelles, two deer, and a bunch of others I didn't recognize.

"I don't get it," Jake said. "What's with the boat?"

Dad shook his head. "That's not just any boat. That's—"

And then I recognized it, just like the pictures from Sunday school. "An ark?" I asked. "Is that . . ."

Dad slowly nodded.

"Why would the Machine project that?" Jake asked.

Gita sighed. "It was the second relic of our experiment. We had placed it on the pedestal for preliminary adjustments last night. Apparently the Machine did not entirely shut down."

We stared speechless as a pair of camels sauntered past.

"The animals must sense its presence," Dad said.

Gita nodded. "As with our own senses, they are fooled into believing it is real."

"Look out!" Jake yelled.

We looked up and ducked as a pair of vultures flew low overhead, followed by a couple eagles, geese, ducks, doves, and beyond them, pairs and pairs of birds, every type you could imagine, the sky growing thick with them.

And not just the sky. The ground was also beginning to

swarm. All sorts of creepy-crawlies—lizards, snakes, bugs. Each and every one of them heading right for camp!

"This is terrible," Ibrahim exclaimed. "We shall be overrun. We shall be—"

He was interrupted by a bone-chilling

HOWLLL . . .

We spun around to see two desert wolves racing toward us.

"Be cool!" Isaac shouted. "They're not interested in us. Just ignore them."

We tried our best to stay calm as they ran past, so close I could have reached out and touched (or been eaten by) them. They were followed by a pair of spotted hyenas, then two scrawny jackals, and more and more animals coming from every direction.

"We must contact Dr. Robbie," Gita said. "He will help us resolve the problem with the Machine."

"He's a little indisposed," Dad said. "Until we get him out of jail, we've got to handle this on our own. Come on!" He started down the hill. "And watch your step!"

We traipsed after him, trying our best not to stomp on anything . . . or let anything stomp on us.

"This is all your fault!" Isaac shouted at Ibrahim.

"Why do you say such a thing?"

"You're the one who was supposed to shut down the Machine."

"As you can see, it did not shut down."

"My point, exactly."

"Listen, my friend—"

"I'm not your friend. I'll *never* be your friend."

And so the bickering continued as more bugs, birds, and animals of every kind joined us. Or we joined them. Yes, sir, it had become quite the parade, with us in the middle.

When I looked over to Jake, I saw he was already grinning. As usual, I knew exactly what was on his mind. If we thought things were over, we couldn't be more wrong. Between this wild country, its incredible history, the camp's strange people, the Machine, and all the haywire inventions, it looked like our adventures had barely begun . . .

PARENT CONNECTION

REMEMBER:

We know that all things work together for the good of those who love God: those who are called according to His purpose. —Romans 8:28

READ:

In the story of Joseph (Genesis 37–41), you'll see that he has a lot more in common with Jennifer and Jake than names that start with *J*. Just like the siblings in *Truth Seekers*, Joseph has a rough start to his young life and finds himself in a foreign country and uncertain circumstances. But in the end Joseph learns that—no matter how bad or unfair things seem—you can always trust God to work things out for your good.

THINK:

1. In what ways are Jennifer and Jake like Joseph in the Bible?
2. What advice did Gita have to help Jennifer trust God?

3. Has there ever been a time when you wondered if God could be trusted? What happened?
4. Name one area in your life where you need to trust God right now.
5. What advice or Bible verses will help you to trust Him?

Do:

A TRUST Acronym
1. Grab a piece of paper or notepad and something to write with.
2. Write the letters, T, R, U, S, and T vertically down the page.
3. Now, using your Bible, advice from *Truth Seekers*, or other wisdom, think of some truths that will help you to trust in God when things seem uncertain.
4. List them, using the letters from the word TRUST to begin each phrase. (For instance, for R you could use "Romans 8:28.")
5. Decorate or embellish, if you'd like. But be sure to keep this reminder where you can see it or find it easily.

Trusting God to do what's best isn't always easy.

But He has promised that He's always working for our good.

BILL MYERS

TRUTH SEEKERS

CHOICES

MAY 2014

IT BEGINS ALL OVER AGAIN. . . .

BILL MUIR and ALEX KENDRICK

Finding it is only the beginning

THE LOST MEDALLION

The Adventures of Billy Stone

A story of lost treasure and adventure… and of discovering the power of the One who created us all.

The son of an archaeologist finds the lost medallion his father had been seeking and is transported back in time with his best friend for an adventure that will change his life forever.

Available Now

A New & Exciting Adventure

BASH and the Pirate Pig

by BURTON W. COLE
...ations by TOM BANCROFT

When a cranky, video game-loving city kid named Beamer has to spend the summer on a farm with his country cousin Bash, he suspects it's gonna stink—and not just because there's a pig involved. But, through Bash's adventures with his "Fishin' and Farmin' book" (The Bible) it just might lead Beamer to the coolest Discovery of all.

Available Fall 2013